The Mysteries of Shadows Creek

THE MYSTERIES OF SHADOWS CREEK

THE NEW NEIGHBORHOOD

J'NAI COACH

Tandem Light Press
PUBLISHING, INSPIRATION, CHANGE.

LAWRENCEVILLE, GA

Tandem Light Press
950 Herrington Rd.
Suite C128
Lawrenceville, GA 30044

Tandem Light Press paperback edition

ISBN: 9781732830899
Library of Congress Control Number: 2019951811

This is a work of fiction. Names, characters, businesses, places, events, locales, and incidents are either the products of the author's imagination or used in a fictitious manner. Any resemblance to actual persons, living or dead, or actual events is purely coincidental.

PRINTED IN THE UNITED STATES OF AMERICA

I would like to dedicate this book to my parents and my best friend Abbi for being there with me through this journey, and my two puppies for helping me with stressful times.

SUNS CREEK DAILY

In our news today, the young, teenage Jallen McSalle talks about his experience when he walked into the forest of shadows, a frightening place in Suns Creek where the sun doesn't shine and leaves a chill down your spine. Mr. McSalle found something that no one could explain. His description makes everyone cower in fear.

"I walked into the forest, curious to see what was in there despite all of the warnings I was given. As I walked in a chill ran down my spine. It was silent, and nerve wracking. The trees were all dead, and the air was all damp, and it was hard to breathe."

McSalle's words are stuttered, clearly shaken by his experience in the forest. His back hunched, and covered in dirt, he adds,

"I saw a dark figure and I decided to walk toward it, as my curiosity got the best of me. As I walked toward it, two piercing white eyes were glancing back at me, and I should've ran when I had the chance. Startled, I jumped back slightly and kept walking. That's when the creature screeched as loud as it could and came at me full speed. I ran as fast as I could, trying to run away but it was able to get a few scratches by trying to grab me."

McSalle unravels the bandages on his arms and shows us. There is still blood everywhere on his arms and it seems severely damaged.

"I never want to go in that forest ever again," he declares.

The forest of shadows is no longer accessible to any of the residents of Suns Creek. There is a wired fence around the forest so no one will be able to go in there even if you try. If you find yourself near the forest, I suggest you turn back while you still can.

CHAPTER ONE
I FALL INTO A HOLE

HELLO THERE, MY name is Jani Topia. I live in a neighborhood called Suns Creek with my confidant and roommate, Autumn Karson. I'm not a normal, everyday person like you people at home. I have one green eye and one eye with no color whatsoever, but I don't like to talk about it much. Doctors have tested me to figure out why my eyes are that way but couldn't find anything. After a while, they gave up and said there was nothing wrong with me, that I just have heterochromia. Heterochromia is simply having two different eye colors, but I don't believe it for a second—one of my eyes has *no* color at all, yet I can see perfectly clear out of it.

My father passed away a long time ago due to being very sick, and my mother passed just recently for the same reason. Everyone thinks I'm a very strange child, only because my parents were very strange as well. Before my parents passed my father was an engineer. He made gadgets that didn't have an important purpose. He once made a machine that could chop wood for us, even though we had no use for it. He also made a mechanical hound because he didn't want a real one. He always told stories about mythical creatures and terrifying monsters, and everyone called him insane for telling nonsense stories.

My mother worked in a flower shop, which you might think isn't strange at all because a lot of people work at flower shops, but the only flowers she ever sold were red roses. People always criticized her for her choice of flowers, but she didn't mind. Ever since my mother died, I have been fond of red roses. Once my father left us, it had just been her and I planting roses, but when she left, I was in a state of grief, in which I could no longer plant anymore roses.

That was when I met my friend Autumn Karson. She never judges a soul, is overprotective, and a huge nerd. One night, we stayed indoors due to the conspicuous weather. The gray clouds covered up the entire sky, and the rain poured so hard that no one even dared to drive on the roads. You couldn't hear anything except the sound of heavy rain hitting the solid pavement. Not even the mechanical hound that I kept outside made a sound from where he stayed, inside of his little doghouse. While all of this was happening, Autumn and I watched movies to pass the time, and as usual, Autumn had the Suns Creek newspaper on her. She read it every day and re-read it every night. I always told her that it's trash and unhealthy, but she ignored me when I said that, coming up with a smart remark in response.

"Look at this," she said, "it's says that a teenaged boy named Jallen McSalle walked into the forest and a dark figure started to screech and chase after him. Isn't that terrifying?"

"Why wouldn't that be terrifying?" I asked.

"Does that mean there are other things in that forest," I wondered to myself. I have heard many stories of the creatures that live in that forest from my father, though I had never been able to believe them.

As I thought about the forest, Autumn walked to the window and looked outside at the storm. Without hesitation, she gasped and called me over. I walked over and peeked out the window, looked at the forest, and couldn't believe my eyes. The forest hadn't been affected by the storm at all. The trees were perfectly still, and the rain fell everywhere except for the forest. Thorns were wrapped around almost every tree.

"Now it's really terrifying" Autumn remarked. "Let's just watch the movie."

We sat on the couch watching the movie worried about what was happening to Suns Creek, our beloved neighborhood. I walked into the kitchen to find something to eat for dinner, but I couldn't really find anything that would fill anyone up.

"I'm going out to the store to find something to eat," I called to Autumn, who sat on the couch trying to clear the smudge off her glasses.

"Okay, but stay safe! The weather is terrible out there!" she replied from the couch.

I grabbed my coat and headed out with my umbrella to the grocery store. On the way there, I took a glance at our animatronic hound. He was asleep in his little house. The sidewalks were soaked and every step I took was like splashing into a puddle. The air was humid and the only sound you could hear was the sound of rain hitting the ground. I checked our mailbox like I did every day. A bill, bill, another bill, a letter to me, and another bill. I never got letters from anyone because people were usually too scared to talk to me. I never really left the house unless I truly had to. I opened the envelope and saw the words in bold letters.

COME TO SHADOWS FOREST OR IT WILL KILL YOU AS SOON AS IT SEES YOU! DO NOT TELL ANYONE ELSE ABOUT THIS MESSAGE. DO NOT PANIC. STAY CALM.

I read the letter over and over, just to make sure what I saw was true. This just had to be a prank, right? I read the note again. It said to go to the forest of shadows. Is that what the forest was called? I never really cared for it. I looked at the forest, which was still unaffected by the storm, thinking about what I should do in this horrible and terrifying situation. I hesitated, then ran to the forest curious, and hoping that nothing would come to hurt me. The chain links weren't in good condition so there was a hole that was large enough for me to fit through. I knew that it was careless, and I should probably have reported this letter to the police, but I wasn't thinking.

As I ran into the forest, the rain stopped instantly. I saw something that made me stop in my tracks. Right there was a giant figure, with piercing white eyes, staring right at me. It didn't do anything but stare. I backed away slowly, hoping that it wouldn't charge right for me. The dead leaves cracked underneath my feet as I walked. It stared for a while, then screeched, and barreled at me in full speed, without stopping. I ran as fast as I could, trying to head back home, but it seemed as if there was no way back.

I kept running. I wasn't fast enough to outrun it, though. It grabbed my arm, and all I could hear was an ear pitching screech. It threw me down a hole—a giant hole—and it flew away as I fell into the dark abyss. I couldn't think…I couldn't even make a sound. I only fall. When I reached the bottom, I hit the ground so hard things became a blur, my head felt like it was floating, and I couldn't move. Before I lost consciousness, I saw a face staring right at me. It was a girl, except she didn't look like a normal girl—she had blue skin, and Prussian-blue hair tied up into a long ponytail, and everything she wore was different shades of blue. She had no irises in her eyes, which was creepy. I couldn't say anything—all I could do was stare.

She gazed at me and mumbled, "Of course something like this has to happen while I'm on break today."

Then, with one final look I finally passed out.

CHAPTER TWO
I MEET SHAFTY & DANIEL

"AM I DEAD?" I asked myself, expecting no one to answer.

"No, you're not dead but I could end your suffering if you want me to," said a sarcastic and calm voice.

Startled by someone answering, I opened my eyes to see the blue girl I saw before I passed out. I then blurted out the first question that came to my mind without thinking, which came off sort of rude.

"Why do you have no irises?"

She looked at me for a moment and said, "Why do you have one green eye and one without any color?"

"I was born this way," I answered, feeling bad for asking the question about her eyes first.

"Which is exactly why I have no irises," she retorted.

"You have no irises because I was born with two different eyes?" I asked, sarcastically and jokingly.

"No, because I was…oh." She stopped her sentence and looked at me annoyed, realizing my joke. "Ha, very funny."

I looked around and realized something—I was no longer in Suns Creek. First, I got this strange letter from an anonymous person, then, I was chased by a giant dark figure, and lastly, I was thrown down a hole, and ended up in a strange place, where I meet this terrifying, blue girl with no irises.

There were dead, black trees everywhere with dead roses around them, and the sky was blood red. The ground was an even darker shade of red, and hazardous thorns were everywhere. Everyone here was different shades of blue and seemed to live normal lives. I wondered where I was, and who was this girl?

As If she read my mind she responded, "My name is Shafty and my last name is not important to the likes of you. You're in our neighborhood called Shadows Creek, and I was the one who sent you the letter about the forest."

So, *she* was the one who sent the letter about something coming to kill me…I was thrown down a hole to another neighborhood? All of this was confusing, and I still needed time to process the information I was given. She seemed like the type that didn't have time for any jokes.

"Why did you send me the letter?" I asked. "Who's coming to kill me and why do they want to kill me?"

"Suns Creek and Shadows Creek are the only connecting neighborhoods on the planet," she said.

"What are connecting neighborhoods?" I asked.

"Connecting neighborhoods are two neighborhoods that are connected to one another—I thought the phrase *connecting neighborhoods* was pretty clear," she responded. "Anyway, the two neighborhoods are connected to each other. One is the innocent neighborhood, where nothing happens, and then there is the other, where there is nothing but trouble. Suns Creek is filled with peaceful humans, while Shadows Creek is filled with terrifying monsters, or as we like to call them, shadows. Every seventy-four years a shadow and a human from Suns Creek are born at the exact same time. The shadows have killed their doubles over the years, and we try to stop them from killing anyone else, but we fail every time, and the shadows get stronger."

I wasn't sure what to think about what was happening. There was a shadow coming to kill me.

"So, it's coming to kill me now," I asked, worried.

"Not if we can help it," Shafty said. "It's 1953 and we have more technology to use against them. We have a plan to keep you safe, or else we will die as well if this keeps up."

"Why would you die?" I asked, curious.

"Everyone in this place is also connected to the roses of this place. If every rose in this place dies, we will die as well, and the shadows will move to Suns Creek and take over. So, we are trying to avoid that happening."

"That thing in the forest," I started, "was that my shadow?"

"Yes. It wanted to kill you, but it dropped you by accident when you wouldn't stop squirming like an idiot."

I was so relieved that it dropped me, but was not relieved that it was still coming for me, and that I was just called an idiot.

"So anyway, before we start our plan to keep you and the world safe, my friend made cookies, would you like any?"

I looked at her, smirking. "You're the nicest thing on Earth, aren't you?"

She rolled her eyes and I followed her to her house.

Once we got there, I realized that this was not your average house, it was a mansion! It was creepy and terrifying, but oddly beautiful. It was a large, white house, with dead roses surrounding it. Thorns were everywhere, but they formed a path to the entrance. There was a pathway to the door, and the door, itself was pure gold.

We went inside to the kitchen and sat at the table. A guy walked in with freshly baked snickerdoodle cookies. When I looked at him, I noticed he also had blue skin, blue hair that looked like it was well-groomed, wore everything blue, and had no iris in his eyes. He seemed sweet and talked with a soothing voice.

"Hi there, my name is Daniel," he said. "Would you like some cookies? I baked them fresh—straight out of the oven."

"Yes please!" I said, starving because I never made it to the store for groceries. If there was anything I missed, it was my mother's homemade cookies. They were the best things I ever tasted. I always watched her bake the cookies, and I used to eat the cookie dough when her back was turned. I tried one of the cookies and was surprised by the taste. The cookies tasted *exactly* like the ones my mother made!

"Does it taste the same?" Daniel asked. I looked at him, confused.

"Does it taste like the cookies your mother made?" Daniel asked with a warm smile.

I glanced at him, wondering how he knew her, and how he knew she baked cookies.

As if he knew what I was thinking he said, "When a shadow is coming for its next victim, the information about the victim is transmitted to our computers."

I cringed at the word victim.

"You know all of my information?" I asked. "So, you already know my name then?"

"Yes, your name is Jani Marie Topia," Daniel answered.

I was a bit disturbed that they had all my information in a computer, but after all that happened that day, I just wished I was back home, living my normal life, without anything trying to kill me. So, I just went back to eating cookies.

I yawned, feeling very tired with all that happened, and needed to find somewhere to sleep.

Daniel looked at me and smiled, "Would you like a place to sleep? We have an extra room if you're tired."

I looked at him and nodded. They seemed like very nice people, but I was still a little paranoid about sleeping there. I mean, who wouldn't be if you were just told that something was coming to kill you? Shafty gave me some of her pajamas, which were all blue, of course, and went to sleep. I went to the room they provided for me and slept. That's when I had the dream.

Chapter Three
DREAMS

"WHY DID YOU *run away?" a dark, raspy voice asked. "I just wanted to be your friend. I wouldn't have hurt you."*

I looked around and saw that I was back home with Autumn.

"We could all be friends if you just come to me," the voice said again.

I looked around, trying to see where the voice was coming from, and I saw the shadow that I had seen in the forest, standing before me. I tried to speak, but couldn't say a word. It wanted to be my friend?! Like I was going to believe that it wanted to be my friend after it just screeched, grabbed and dropped me down a hole.

The shadow approached closer and closer, until I was face to face with it. It smiled, and said in a dark voice, "I guess we can't be friends after all."

It screeched and grabbed me by the neck, strangling me. I saw Autumn in the distance calling my name and looking for me. She must have been worried sick that I'm wasn't there. I couldn't breathe and was starting to gag. The creature's sharp claws swung down as it—

"JANI!"

I was woken up with Shafty by my side, shaking me vigorously.

"What happened?" she asked, looking worried.

"Nothing," I said, not wanting to think about the dream I just had. It seemed so real to me.

"Come on," Shafty said, changing the subject. "Daniel made breakfast."

We walked to the kitchen and sat at the table. Daniel came in wearing a "Kiss the Cook" apron.

"I made pancakes, waffles, eggs, bacon, and milk!" he said happily.

As we ate, we talked about what we were going to do after breakfast. I was too busy thinking about what happened in the dream last night. The shadow wanted me to be her friend, then she decided not to be my friend, then she choked me. It felt so real to me, but I had to keep telling myself it wasn't—it was just a dream.

Daniel said he was going to do some research about how to stop the shadow from coming for me, starting with a book called *The Rose on Fire*. Meanwhile, Shafty said that we had to come up with a disguise to make me fit in with the others. How could they give me a disguise when all they ever wear is blue? She then smirked, which gave me a bad feeling.

"How am I going to fit in with the others?" I asked, suspiciously.

"You'll see, and you'll love the outcome."

Daniel looked up from his book, smiled, and said, "We are going to make you blue, like us."

CHAPTER FOUR
A LIVING BLUEBERRY

BLUE?! WHY WERE they going to turn me blue? As a matter of fact, *how* were they going to make me blue? Was that even possible?

"How, and why are you going to make me blue, exactly?" I asked.

"Well if you didn't know," Daniel started, "colloidal silver makes the skin blue. This was a product invented by your father. Down here everyone is a different shade of blue. In this case, you would be a blue-gray color."

I couldn't believe it. They were going to make me a living blueberry. I saw Shafty get up and grab a carton that said *Colloidal Silver* written on the side. She gave it to me and told me to pour it all over myself. She also gave me a pair of clothes that looked exactly like the ones I came in with when I first met them, except they were blue. A blue sweater, blue shorts, a blue bow, and a blue scarf. I went into the bathroom and got started making myself blue.

After a few hours, I was completely blue. I looked

in the mirror and didn't see Jani Topia, but another person staring right back at me, who just looked like her and a blueberry mixed together. I went over to Daniel and Shafty, who waited for me at the door.

"Want to go out and eat for dinner?" Daniel asked.

I nodded and we drove in his car to a restaurant named, *Red Roses*. Does everything here have to deal with roses, I wondered.

We went inside and sat at a table and ordered a pepperoni pizza.

"Will the shadow recognize me?" I asked while I took a big bite of the pizza, which tasted amazing by the way.

"Don't say that out loud!" Shafty said. "Others can hear you speak. Anyway, it can recognize you, but others can't, so we have to be extra careful when we go in public."

After a few minutes, we talked about other things and ate our pizza. I was starting to like it here, but I still missed home. Then, we heard a loud scream, and turned to see something terrible. I almost had a major heart attack. The shadow was right there, looking at me, all the way on the other side of the restaurant. It screeched so loudly that everyone in the restaurant covered their ears. Then it charged right for me. Everyone in the restaurant started running in different directions. It tried to grab Shafty, but it missed and grabbed our pizza, then threw it across the room, screeching louder and louder.

"Come on, now," I said, "Who doesn't like pizza?"

"Now is not the best time for jokes," Shafty yelled.

We ran as fast as we could out of the restaurant into a small field. It was dark outside, and the sky was pitch black. It smelled terrible. The dead and dry roses were crumbling beneath our feet. As we ran, the shadow was getting closer and closer. I saw Daniel trying to pull a flashlight out of his pocket. He flashed the light at the shadow, and it screeched louder than it ever had before. I was starting to lose vision, and I couldn't run any longer, but I had to keep going. My heart started pounding harder and harder. My vision was starting to become worse, and I began slowing down.

"Come on Jani! Keep running!"

I thought that was Daniels voice, but wasn't quite sure. I stopped running and collapsed. Suddenly, I felt a sharp pain in my leg, then I was knocked out.

Chapter Five
THE ROSE SHORTAGE

I WOKE UP in a white room, wearing an oxygen mask. I looked around and saw that I was in a hospital. I looked down and saw that my leg was wrapped in bandages. Daniel and Shafty were asleep beside me. The shadow must have hurt my leg badly, because it hurt in a way that I have never felt before. I decided to do the only thing I could do right then, and sleep.

"Do you really think they care about you?" the voice asked. "They don't care about you at all, they just want to keep you safe, so they don't die."

This couldn't be happening, I thought. I was having another dream with the shadow, in complete darkness.

"Your friend stopped me with a flashlight, and that was very painful. Don't think you can stop me Jani Topia, I always find a way," the shadow warned.

I was now in the hospital again. Daniel and Shafty were both sleeping. Except, I was still dreaming. The shadow was also in the room. It walked over to Daniel and took the flashlight out of his pocket, smiled, and disappeared.

I woke up and saw that Daniel and Shafty were awake, too.

"I could've sworn it was in my pocket earlier," Daniel said, confused.

With the mask over my face, I couldn't talk to them, but there was so much I wanted to say to them about what just happened. The doctor walked in the room and started talking to the others like I wasn't even there.

"She will not be able to walk like she used to for a while," the doctor started. "Be careful with her leg."

I watched as the conversation went on. I wouldn't be able to walk like I used to until I got better—meaning it would be a lot harder to run away from the shadow.

Daniel carried me out of the hospital and put me in a wheelchair. We walked down the road, not saying a single word. The road was filled with dead roses everywhere. Did that many people die, for there to be so many dead roses? We sat in silence for a while until it was broken when Daniel and Shafty started coughing and sneezing.

"Why are we sick all of a sudden?" Daniel asked.

"I have no idea why but—"

Shafty was interrupted by the screams of many people in terror. Daniel and Shafty ran as fast as they could while pushing me with them.

"What is going on here?" Shafty asked.

A man turned his head. He was pale in the face, baby blue to be exact, and looked terrified. He said, "There's only a few roses left in the garden! We are trying our best to grow more, but it's taking forever! Haven't you heard? We're all going to die!" He started running away crying, saying he has a wife had kids that he's going to lose.

Shafty and Daniel started turning pale. They pushed me toward their house. Once we got inside, they locked every window and door. The last rose was now barricaded with thorns and lights everywhere so the shadow wouldn't even dare get near it. Everyone else was very sick and in their homes, terrified, saying goodbye to their families.

"We need to find a way to stop that shadow once and for all." Shafty said.

"I do have one idea," Daniel started, "but it's very risky."

"Ok what's the plan?" Shafty asked.

"I think that we should follow Jani's shadow, to find the person creating these terrible creatures."

"That's actually a good idea." Shafty said in agreement. "All we need to do is gather up some people"

"The risky part," Daniel started, "is taking Jani with us." Both looked at me waiting for an answer.

"Let's do it," I said.

CHAPTER SIX
FREE WEAPONS AND FIGHTING SHADOWS

FINALLY, ABLE TO walk on my leg, Shafty, Daniel, and I ran to a weapons shop. My leg felt so much better than it did before

"I can't stand this place," Shafty said.

"Why not?" I asked

"You'll see once we get there…"

"Come on Shafty, he's not that bad!" Daniel said.

"Who are they talking about and why do they even have a weapons shop here in Shadows creek?" I wonder to myself.

We walked inside and saw a man at the counter. Right when we entered, an arrow hit the wall narrowly avoiding Shafty's head.

"Hi Daniel. Hello feisty—I mean Shafty!"

Shafty clenched her fist tight and looked away.

"Hello William," Daniel said.

William looked at me, then started walking toward me. I almost bolted, but he grabbed my arm so tight it hurt.

"Who is this trash?"

"That's just our friend Jani! Just an ordinary person from Shadows Creek, like us!" Daniel said quickly and nervously.

"I hope she isn't like your other so-called friend over there," he said with clear hate toward Shafty

"What good do you get from torturing me? I don't understand it. What's done is done. I don't work here anymore, and that's what you wanted, right?" Shafty yelled, with a look on her face that made Daniel and I stand back, frightened by the sudden outburst. Without a warning, she punched William right in the face, hard. He lay on the floor, knocked out, with a bruise on his nose. I was about to say something, but Daniel looked at me and shook his head, telling me not to—it would only make things worse.

We followed Shafty into the back, stepping over the knocked-out body on the ground.

"What's up with her?" I whispered to Daniel.

"Shafty used to work in this store with William. Shafty won employee of the year and William didn't. The boss of this place clearly favored Shafty more than William which made him jealous. He tried his best to get his boss's attention, but it never worked. On the other hand, Shafty didn't care about getting the attention or anything like that. One day, she even tried to get her boss to go over to William and focus on him instead of her, but it never worked."

William was jealous of Shafty gaining all the attention. It started to make sense. Shafty didn't seem like the type to work in a store like this.

"She ended up quitting the job because she got bored and was irritated by the boss's attention. If I knew any better, I honestly think that he might have had feelings toward her, and Shafty can't stand people who do," Daniel said, scratching his chin.

We walked into a room filled with weapons. There weren't many weapons in here, just a few that were very unorganized, and a few that clearly didn't work. For someone who wanted to impress their boss, William surely didn't do a good job taking care of the place. There was one item that caught my eye. It was covered in roses and said, "Roses Regeneration." It was beautiful. The whole weapon was slightly large, and it was a silver color with golden rims. It didn't come with anything, such as a case or any ammunition. It just had a small button on the side and nothing else. I grabbed it as Shafty and Daniel picked their own.

We walked out and saw that it was very crowded outside in the streets. Some people were crying next to each other, and others were flat out screaming in terror. People around us were wheezing, coughing, sneezing and groaning due to being sick. Shafty and Daniel started to cough and wheeze, too, which made me worried, considering what they had told me earlier about their connections with roses.

In the distance I saw it running as fast as it could. My shadow was heading toward a tunnel in the back of a building. It didn't look happy, either. We followed it inside of the tunnel, making sure not to make a sound so we didn't get caught. That would make things worse than it already was.

At the end of the tunnel it cut off, making the tunnel seem like a cliff over a giant cave-like place down below. I imagined the cave was filled with thorns and more dead roses. There were shadows everywhere, and the lights were dimmed so you could barely see anything. We watched as my shadow walked up to a very tall figure.

"Well did you kill her yet? I'm still waiting here, and I don't see anyone here before me," the tall figure said, sounding impatient and cruel.

"Not yet, but I am very close, Dr.Cruser."

They were talking for a while, about me, apparently. All of a sudden, we heard a screeching…

"I found some eavesdroppers!" Every shadow in the entire cave looked at us and screeches filled the entire room.

Daniel stood up, surprisingly without ears covered from the loud noises, and threw a ball looking figure as hard as he possibly could. The entire room filled up with a blinding light. A few shadows disintegrated quickly. They must have been weak, because a lot more shadows didn't seem affected by the light. Shafty shot something at one of the shadows and it disintegrated as well, just like the others. While Shafty and Daniel fought the shadows, I pulled out the rose generator. I tried to shoot it, but nothing happened. Nothing at all. I couldn't do anything but stay close to the others while they fought.

What is this for if I can't even use it, I thought to myself. It must be broken or something.

Daniel handed me a few of his weapons, and I started throwing them as hard as I could around the room. Ear piercing screeches filled the room even louder, which made us stop for a while.

Suddenly, I felt a shadow grab my right leg and toss me across the room. The sudden movement caused me to lose my thoughts for a while, until I finally looked up and saw that the shadow had started charging for me. I saw a flashlight right beside me. I shined the light at the shadow, and it disappeared just like some of the others. I ran back to Shafty and Daniel, leaving the flashlight behind without thinking.

After what seemed like forever, the only shadow left was my shadow. Dr. Cruser must have left while we were fighting, which was another problem that we'd going to have to deal with later. The shadow that was going after me all this time and who tried to kill me multiple times looked at me but wasn't smiling an evil smile. It looked, remorseful in a way.

In the most normal human voice, it said, "There's a lot of strange mysteries here in Shadows Creek, Jani." It picked up the flashlight that I left on the ground in the corner of the room. "Be careful with it though, you just might regret it someday." It flashed itself with the flashlight disintegrating instantly. We all just stood in silence, not saying a word.

CHAPTER SEVEN
MY NEW HOME

IT WAS OVER. Dr. Cruser escaped, my shadow was defeated, and there was still only one rose left, which was saddening.

"What are we going to do about the roses?" Daniel asked, looking weak and frail.

I looked at the rose regenerator, when I turned it over I saw the words 'made by Charlie Topia'—that was my father's name… I remembered it now. This was my father's anniversary gift to my mother. My mom grew many roses, so my father had made a machine that made dead roses grow back instantly.

I shot the device and suddenly, a ray of light shot out of the machine. Dead roses everywhere grew back to normal—bright red and beautiful.

"This is breathtaking." Daniel said.

"Now the roses will never die again with this device." Shafty said.

Afterwards, our group had celebrated at Daniel and Shafty's house for one of Daniel's homecooked dinners. We talked and laughed, as we felt the relief of our problems being solved.

"I guess you have to go back home, now, don't you?" Daniel said, sounding slightly disappointed.

I thought for a while. I didn't want to leave this place. I loved this place, and its people, but I also missed my roommate Autumn. I wished I could send her a card or something like that. As much as I miss Autumn, I just knew that this was going to be my new home. I was not leaving this place.

"Is there any way I could leave a postcard back to Autumn?" I asked.

"Aren't you going back?" Daniel asked, noticing how long I was quiet.

"I decided I wanted to stay here with you guys!" I said with a smile.

Daniel looked very excited. Even Shafty looked like she wanted to smile, but all I got was a small smirk—good enough for me.

I sent a card to Suns Creek explaining how I found a new place to live and how I was very sorry I left Autumn alone. I received a card in return saying that it was ok, and that should I should send cards occasionally. Autumn said she wasn't alone either, because after a few days she sent a card saying she made a new friend when she went to the store, and they decided to live together as roommates. I didn't tell her about anything that happened here in Shadows Creek, though. I had to tell her that I just left the neighborhood, and went somewhere far away. I hoped she wouldn't want to visit at all, but she wasn't the traveling type anyway.

I thought for a moment about what my shadow said. What strange mysteries?

Why should I be careful? You know what, I wasn't going to worry about it. Everything was better than it was before and that's all that mattered. I had my own bedroom now in Daniel and Shafty's house, and we all went to a small clothing store to buy me the things I needed so I could stay here.

I still had a few mysteries to solve, though. Why were my eyes the way they were? Where did Dr. Cruser go, and what unfolds next in Shadows Creek?

Just then, Shafty walked over to me holding a letter.

"Jani," she said, with a nervous voice, which was slightly nerve wracking, "Your parents aren't dead."

CHAPTER EIGHT
MEETING LIAM AND SURPRISING SECRETS

"YOUR PARENTS AREN'T dead," Shafty said.

"What are you talking about? My parents died a long time ago," I said.

Shafty handed me a letter with red writing on it.

"Read this, your mother sent it."

I took the letter out of her hand and read it while she walked into a different room to talk to Daniel.

I know this may surprise you but, your father and I aren't dead. Your father is still missing, but I know where he is. I really need your help Jani. Come meet me at Holbeck Garden. We'll discuss everything there. I'm sorry we left you thinking that we were dead. I hope you can forgive us.'

This couldn't be a real letter could it? Well it *was* in her handwriting. I was having mixed emotions about this. I was surprised that they were alive, angry that they lied to me, disappointed that my father was still missing. Mother said she knew where he was, so maybe we could all go looking for him later… She did say she was sorry for leaving me. So, could I even forgive her after she left me alone all of those years? Where was this Holbeck Garden, and why did she want to meet there? I didn't even know how to get to the place. I really should have been happy that I got this letter. My mother was alive, and I was able to see her again. So why did I feel hesitant about it?

I looked over at Shafty and Daniel who were having a conversation in another room. While they were distracted, I ran out of the room as fast as I could without stopping. I didn't know where I was going, but I kept running, hoping to find Holbeck garden. I could hear Shafty and Daniel shouting behind me, but I just ignored them. I had to keep going until I found my mother.

It was starting to get dark and I didn't know where I was going. I stopped, needing to ask for directions. I paused in front of a man wearing an all blue flannel, who had short hair, and was so tall he could possibly be a giant, and asked,

"Excuse me, do you know where Holbeck Garden is?"

He glanced at me with a worried look on his face. He started fidgeting nervously.

"Why would you want to go there? That place is treacherous."

I looked at him confused. "What's wrong with Holbeck Garden?"

He grabbed my shoulders, his face looked very anxious—you could tell he was frightened by the place. I'm not really fond of being touched so I brushed his hands off my shoulders.

"You can't go in that Garden! Especially at this time of day! Do you know how many people are deceased in that garden?"

"Deceased? My mother is in that garden waiting for me! She could be in trouble!" I shouted.

"Then let me go with you," he said, "I don't want to see another person lose their life by going in there."

We walked into the garden and looked around for my mother. The garden didn't look as I expected it would. Every flower here was dead, the trees were dead, and there was dust everywhere. There were more gravestones than anything else here. Why would she pick this garden, did she know how dangerous it was?

"What's your name?" I asked, wanting to break the uncomfortable silence.

After a while he finally responded, "My name is Liam, what about you?" "

"I'm Jani, I'm kind of new here if you haven't noticed," I said.

"Well, not every person would want to go into this garden, especially at night," he said, with a small smile.

I was going to respond, until we heard a loud, ear piercing, scream.

"Stay here," Liam whispered, as he ran to the location of the noise.

I wasn't just going to stand here while my mother could be in danger. Following him, I hid behind a tree. Liam started walking around and examining the fountain. He looked inside and gasped.

"A dead body," he whispered to himself.

A lady started walking towards Liam, holding an axe. She wasn't even blue. She had jet-black hair covering her face, and caramel skin, just like me before the others turned me blue. That couldn't have been who I thought it was, could it? No, of course not, that wasn't possible. The lady grabbed Liam's arm, and tried to swing the axe, but Liam had faster reflexes and grabbed it.

"Who are you?" he asked the lady.

"None of your business!" she yelled back.

That voice was too familiar. I had heard it before, but I just didn't know where. I had to stop whoever this was from killing Liam. He knew a lot about this place, and I wasn't giving up the chance to ask him questions. I grabbed a thick branch from a tree off the ground. As I ran up to the lady, I hit her with all of my strength in the back of her head, which knocked her out.

"Thank you for saving me." Liam said, as he picked up the lady in one of his arms. "We should go somewhere safer. This isn't really a place we should stay."

"We can go see my two friends Shafty and Daniel. They know a lot of things about mysteries and they're the ones who saved me from—"

I stopped talking. I couldn't tell him that I was from Suns Creek. The only ones who knew about that were Shafty and Daniel. No one else knew.

"What were you saying?" Liam said curiously.

"Nothing," I said quickly.

As we walked, I looked at the lady. She looked so familiar, like I'd seen her before.

"Can you move the hair out of her eyes Liam?"

He looked at me, confused, and moved her hair. My heart dropped, and my breathing became heavy. This must be a dream—this can't be real. The woman that I knocked out, in Liam's arms, the one who tried to murder him, the one who sent me a letter wanting me to go to the garden, was my own mother.

Chapter Nine
HERE WE GO AGAIN

WHY WOULD SHE have lied to me? Had she planned on killing me too? What would have happened if it was just me? So many thoughts and emotions are going through my head. Anger, hatred, disappointment. I felt like I was beginning to lose my sanity.

"Are you ok?" Liam asked me.

"Yeah. Here we are."

We stopped in front of the house, and I barely opened the door, and it busted open, only to get a giant hug from Daniel.

"Why did you run off? We were worried about you!" Daniel asked. "I wanted to go after you, but *someone* wouldn't let me," Daniel said as he motioned towards Shafty.

I looked at her and she sighed.

"I knew you were going to come back eventually, so I decided to let you go."

Liam walked in, carrying my mother in his arms. He had to bend down in order to get through the door. Daniel and Shafty just stared at my mother in his arms without saying a word. It was silent for a while.

"Jani can we talk to you alone please?" Shafty asked, not keeping her eyes off my mother.

"Sure, I guess." I said.

I followed them down the hall into Daniel's office. On the way down there, nobody said anything. I was pretty sure I knew what they were going to talk about. My mother in Liam's arms, knocked out. The fact that Liam was even there. Once we got to his office, Daniel and Shafty sat down, and so I decided to take a seat as well.

"So, you know what she's been doing?" Shafty asked calmly.

"No, what did she do?" I asked.

"Well," Daniel started, "The citizens of this neighborhood's, lives are at stake."

"Why is that?" I asked.

"Your mother has been kidnapping, hurting, and also killing the citizens."

My mother, out of all people did that to innocent people? Why would she do that?

"Remember the guy who created all of those shadows that we fought?" Shafty asked.

"Yes, his name was Dr.Cruser." I said, remembering how he tried to kill me with one of his shadow creatures. I had to hide away from the shadows, until we found out that they disintegrated with light. I hadn't seen Dr.Cruser before, though.

"Jani, your mother started working for him. We just found out a while ago when you left," Shafty said.

"She's not very good at hiding evidence, that's for sure." Daniel said, smiling.

We all walked back into the room with Liam, who was sitting in a chair, with my mother tied up to another. Daniel dragged the chair with the unconscious lady to another room and locked it. He then came back and sat with the rest of us.

"Hello, Liam," Daniel said, sounding quite disturbed.

"Hello, Walter," Liam said, equally uncomfortable.

"I don't go by that filthy name anymore, Liam. I respect your change of name, so I would be pleased if you respected mine."

"Oh, I forgot you go by *Daniel* now," Liam said, chuckling with a wide grin.

"Your real name is Walter?" I asked, breaking the unsettling tension between the two. As if I hadn't said anything, Daniel ignored me. Shafty noticed and gave me a look, telling me to keep my mouth shut.

"They were in college together, and have two very different personalities," Shafty whispers to me.

There was an awkward silence for a moment. Everyone is avoided eye contact with each other.

"Just tell us what happened," Shafty said.

Liam and I spent time explaining everything that happened in Holbeck Garden. We explained when we met, hearing screams, finding the body, and knocking out my own mother.

"It's a good thing you brought her here. She has a death sentence at the local prison, and we need her in order to interrogate her." Daniel said.

Liam stood up, and almost left, until Shafty pulled him back in.

"You're working with us now," she said, "You know too much already, and there's a chance that you can tell everyone."

Liam looked at Shafty, clearly puzzled, and sat back down.

"Who said I was going to tell anybody, Shaf?"

Shafty also looked annoyed.

"Don't call me Shaf. And the reason we aren't letting you go is because you're untrustworthy."

"How am I untrustworthy exactly?"

The two kept arguing and eventually, Daniel joined in too. How did this happen? Liam seemed like a nice, albeit giant-like, person. Now that he's arguing with my friends, he seems to be a completely different person. They must have some terrible history together.

Suddenly, a lot of screaming and a crash came from the room my mother was tied up in. We all ran in to the room to see what all the noise was. The chair we tied her in was broken, and the window was shattered, broken glass was all over the floor. On the floor my mother laid there, dead, with a note beside her.

Everyone stood in complete silence with their eyes wide. I walked over to the body and picked up the note that was left on the floor beside her. I read it aloud to the group.

Well done Jani. I never expected you to get this far. You might be astonished that your dearest mother is dead right in front of you. You already know too much, and interrogating her would have given you more information. I couldn't let that happen, now, could I?

Sincerely,

Dr. Cruser

P.S. I have something improved and sturdier than the shadows now. You can come over to the machinery if you want to start this war now, but be warned, I will not lose this time!

The handwriting looked so familiar, but I just couldn't figure it out. I looked at the group after I finished reading, and that's when Daniel spoke, trying to lighten the mood.

"Time for another adventure guys!"

We all looked at Daniel and smiled. If we put our minds to it, maybe we could defeat Dr. Cruser after all, and perhaps find my father in the process.

We left the house with my mother buried in the backyard. Why should I care, I thought. She betrayed me and my father. Besides, Once I found my father, I was going to tell him everything that happened. I'd tell him about falling here, finding this place, fighting the shadows, finding my mother, and then once we defeated Dr.Cruser, I'd tell him about that, too.

CHAPTER TEN
WHERE'S THE HAPPY ENDING?

DANIEL AND SHAFTY were arguing with each other, only because we have to go to the place we got our weapons from last time. Shafty used to work at this weapons store with a guy named William. And because she always made employee of the year, William was jealous of her. Last time we went there, Shafty knocked him out and we had stolen a few weapons.

Once we made it to the store, we saw William at the front desk. He looked over at us with an angry look on his face, his nose bandaged where Shafty punched him.

"If you keep coming to this store, I will have you banned. You broke my nose, and I had to go to the hospital!" He said furiously.

"Save the talk or I'll punch you in the same spot again." Shafty said, annoyed. She walked to the back and came out with random weapons that looked huge. She handed them out to us one by one. My weapon looked awesome! It looked like a bow and arrow, except it was huge and mechanical. It had different settings on it too, and the tip of the arrow could be on fire, conduct electricity, or could just be a regular arrow. I looked on the side and written on it was the name, "Charlie Topia." So this had been made by father as well, then.

"Hey, you can't just steal weapons, you have to pay for them first. This is a classy store!" William yelled.

"You work at a weapons store that barely even has that many weapons in the first place, and it's completely filthy. You have rats and spider webs everywhere, not to mention mold." Liam said with a disgusted look on his face.

Then Daniel spoke, "So how exactly is this place classy?"

"Just take your weapons and please just get out of my store, and never come back." William said, not answering the question.

"You do realize that we are pretty much your only customers, and no one else even wants to come to this store because of your sick attitude and filthy place." Shafty said.

All the others continued arguing while I decided to look around the store without them. They were right, it was very filthy. Some of the weapons were just basic everyday weapons like guns and knives. I walked to the back of the store, only to find a rat eating a moldy sandwich. I watched it for a while, but soon became bored, and left it to enjoy its lunch.

When I return to the group, I saw William on the ground, knocked out with his nose bleeding, and the bandage that was around it, was now covered in his blood.

I looked at Shafty with a concerned face and she noticed me looking at her.

She whispered, "Wasn't me this time."

I looked at Daniel who had his fist clenched and had blood on his knuckles.

"I think we all should probably run," he said.

All of us ran away towards to the direction to the machinery.

"Why am I even with you guys? You guys are psychos and murderers!" Liam yelled while running.

"We aren't murderers, he's just knocked out, and if you keep talking, you'll end up just like him," Shafty said, obviously annoyed with Liam's complaining.

We made it to the machinery building, and the place was huge. I had never seen a place this large before. There were knocked-down, dead trees everywhere. In the front were two guards, except they didn't look human. They looked like two big dog-like creatures, with fur, and their skin was a very dark, navy blue color.

We tried to casually walk over to the guards without saying anything, but one of them stopped us before we could make it in. His voice was deeper than I expected, and it was a little raspy, as well.

"Who are you and what are you doing here? This place is off limits."

"We were told to come here by Dr.Cruser," I said, in fear of the overly large and tall hound.

"Wait a minute, your Charlie Topia's daughter, aren't you?" the other guard said with a surprised look on his face.

How did this *thing* know my father?

"Yes, I am. How do you know my father?" I asked, with a low tone in my voice, trying to sound at least a little intimidating.

"Your father and I go *way* back. He was a great guy, until the change happened," he said, with a disappointing sigh.

"What kind of change? What happened to my father?" I asked, curiously.

"Never mind that. I'll let you guys inside, be careful."

He opened the door to the machinery, and we all walked inside. The way he said "be careful" sounded slightly sarcastic. This was so nerve wracking and caused me to have major anxiety. We looked up at a balcony and saw something no one would ever want to see. Just like to the two guards outside, there were large dog-like creatures surrounding the entire upstairs balcony, except these were much larger than the ones outside. They all stared at us with blank stares on their faces, like they were emotionless.

"Maybe we walked into the wrong machinery?" Liam asked with a weak voice.

"You do realize that this is the only machinery in Shadows Creek, right?" Shafty asked, glancing at Liam. He didn't respond and stayed quiet.

With no warning a booming voice exited out of the speakers, which startled all of us.

"So, you actually made it? That's great to hear! I have been waiting for your arrival, but you can only get to me if you have the strength to defeat all of my savage canines."

We all stared at the speakers, with terrified faces. That voice was extremely familiar to me, I just couldn't put my finger on it. The wild dogs on the balcony jumped down, and charged at us with a movement so quick, it was hard to get a clear look at them. Liam ran back outside before they could even get to him, like a coward. A big one ran towards Shafty, but thankfully she was able to dodge it in time. One of them hit me right in the stomach, and it hit me so hard that I vomited, right on the head of one of the other dogs. The one I vomited on looked confused, looked at me with a disgusted look, then left to fight one of the others. Daniel saw everything that just happened.

He suggested, "Why don't you look for Dr.Cruser while we fight the giant dogs?" I nodded and tried to sneak to the speaker room without being seen, but one of the dogs found me, and blocked my way.

"You're not going anywhere short stack," it said in a weird growling voice. Did it just call me short stack?

"I am five feet and two inches, thank you. I'm not short at all!" I said angrily. Just then, I remembered that I had a bow and arrow. I took it out of the bag that was on my back and aimed it at the dog. It looked at me and laughed.

"You think a small bow and arrow will do me some damage, kid?"

Ignoring the question, I set the arrow to electricity, and the tip of the arrow started lighting up, which was pretty cool. I released it and it hit the dog in the chest. It fell over to its side, started twitching, and freaking out. Smoke started to form around the dog. I walked around it, trying to avoid being electrocuted, and went upstairs, where I made it inside of the speaker room.

When I got in there, I saw a very tall man, sitting at a huge control panel, unaware that I was standing behind him. He looked extremely stressed out for a villain. His hair was a mess, and his back was hunched. He wore a green suit, which made him look slightly professional, and it was to only other color clothing I'd ever seen at Shadows Creek.

On the controls there were labels for each different function. One of them was labeled shadows but was marked with a red "FAILED" over it. That must have been the time where we defeated the shadow creatures once and for all. On his desk there was a lot of clutter. There were large stacks of papers, pencils, pens, and a photo inside of a frame. I wanted to get a closer look, so I quietly walked closer to his desk without being seen. I looked at the picture and almost vomited once again. Why did he have a picture of me and my father? What kind of person would steal family photos from someone? What was wrong with this guy?

"What is wrong with you, and why do you have this?!" I yelled at him, with my bow and arrow pointed at his head.

I must have scared him, because he fell on the floor, and covered his face. I still aimed at his head waited for an answer.

With his face still covered he said, "It's my picture that's why."

I looked at him confused. What could he possibly mean by that when the photo clearly wasn't his? I aimed closer and set the arrow to the fire this time. The tip of the arrow now had a small, raging flame.

"What are you talking about?" I asked.

He slowly lowered his hands and looked at me with wide eyes. I thought I might cry after seeing who he was. First, my own mother betrays me, and now my own father, out of all people, was Dr. Cruser. Could anyone in my family be normal?

"How could you?" I whispered quietly.

This must be the change the guard was talking about outside of the building. He just looked at me and frowned.

"It all started with faking our death Jani. People judged us too much, so we decided to make them feel bad by faking our own deaths. We found this place and decided to live here. Your mother started going on and on about not fitting in and went crazy. Then she became a killer."

"What does that have to do with you becoming a murderer?" I asked with the arrow still aimed at his head.

"Since my own wife went evil, I decided that I should go back to inventing. The people here didn't like my inventions, so I created shadows to teach them a lesson, but you killed all of them. Now I have giant savage canines," he explained, smiling at the end of his explanation.

"I want more answers. Why are you trying to kill me?" I said, angry.

"You were supposed to stay in Suns Creek with your friend Autumn, but you decided to come down here, instead," he said with a stern voice.

"One more question," I started. "Why are my eyes different from others?"

"That's for you to figure out Jani. I can't tell you anything else."

He stood up and went to the control panel. On a screen you could see Shafty and Daniel fighting, and Liam crying in a corner.

"Jani, some secrets are meant to be kept secret, and not shared. Just like Shadows Creek," He said as he walked over to a lever that said *REVERSE* and pulled it. "And I am one of the few people who knows the answers to these secrets." The dogs in the other rooms stopped fighting and ran out of view. Then, the room suddenly smelled of wet dog and blood. "So, that is why I'm going to make sure no one ever finds out the mysteries of Shadows Creek."

I looked at him, confused, and the smell got stronger. The dogs came through the door and all of them jumped on top of Dr. Cruser. I stood there in shock, while the only sound filling the room was the tearing of cloth, and Dr. Cruser screaming. The dogs eventually left the room, acting like I wasn't even there.

I looked over at Dr. Cruser and I almost fainted. His skin and clothes were torn, and there was blood everywhere. I fell to the floor and started to lose consciousness slowly. Before I was completely knocked out, I heard Shafty's and Daniel's voices. They were okay and alive—that's good—but now both of my parents are dead. Unless we could find the people with the secrets of this place, the mysteries of Shadows Creek will never be discovered.

CHAPTER ELEVEN
THIS ISN'T EVEN A REAL HOSPITAL...

I WOKE UP to the sound of beeping, and I opened my eyes to find myself in a hospital. Right above me I could see Liam looking right at me.

"She probably doesn't want you in her face Liam, just saying," Shafty said, looking at me also.

Liam sat down in a chair while a nurse with dark circles under her eyes walked into the room holding a tray. I couldn't quite see what was on the tray but I'm guessed that it was probably nothing. The doctor followed her into the room, wearing a mask and gloves. He was speed walking towards the hospital bed. Once he got to me, he held my eyes open while shining a flashlight right in them, which burned, by the way.

He looked at Shafty and Daniel and asked, "What's wrong with her eyes?"

"What an absurd question to ask," I thought to myself. "You should never point things out on people other than yourself."

"Shafty and I think that it might be complete heterochromia. It's the most logical explanation," Daniel said.

"That can't be it. She has no color in this one, but she does in her other. That's not a normal presentation of heterochromia," The doctor explained while he turned off the flashlight. "Heterochromia is two different eye colors, but she has only one colored eye."

The two just looked at each other confused.

"I thought we were here to stop her from fainting." Liam said.

The doctor ignored him like he didn't say a word and looked at me with a face that was kind of disturbing.

The nurse went over to the doctor and whispered something in his ear, which made the doctor glance over and give me a creepy smirk. The nurse then looked at me with a scrunched-up, angry face. I wondered, did I do something wrong that I'm not aware of?

"I'm going to need the three of you to leave the room, this is going to be private business," the doctor said.

The others hesitantly left the room while I was busy reading the doctor's name tag. His name was Dr. Slaughter—a therapist, phycologist, and surgeon. According to his tag, this place was a psychiatric hospital for people with mental illnesses. This was the opposite of what I needed. I didn't have a mental illness, and we were just trying to stop my fainting right?

The nurse went over to the right side of my bed while the doctor led the others to a different room. He then walked back in and slammed the door shut, locking it in the process, which startled me. The nurse strapped me to the hospital table quickly, without saying a word. I tried to say something, but a large needle was quickly stabbed into my shoulder. This made chills go all over my spine, and my body felt like it was on fire. I tried to scream in pain, but I couldn't say anything. My mouth was extremely numb. I tried kicking my legs to get loose, but the nurse stabbed my right leg so I couldn't feel anything and did the same thing to the left. My entire body felt like I was walking through fire, and the pain was absolutely unbearable. The worse part about the whole thing was that she didn't take out the needles, so they were still stuck in my shoulder and legs. In terror, I asked myself "What is going on and why are they doing this me?"

I started panicking while Dr. Slaughter loomed above me, smiling behind the mask he was wearing on his face.

"They told me that the girl with the strange eyes would come and visit my hospital, and now I have finally gotten a hold of you. Do you know how long I have yearned, waiting for you to arrive?"

I wanted to say something, but I couldn't.

"You're probably wondering why I wanted to see you, and you must have so many questions at the moment," he continued. His face started changing into an expression that made him look annoyed by something.

"My hospital was always on the first page of the newspaper, and the only thing people would ever talk about was Dr. Slaughter's Mental Hospital, the most famous hospital known." His face changed from annoyed to angry. "Once you came around and 'saved' everyone from our shadow issue, everyone turned their attention away from me, and only talked about you and your fame. I no longer have the front page of the newspaper, you do. I'm no longer the main subject in everyone's conversations, you are. Now that you saved everyone, the only thing people ever talk about is the fact that you have two different eye colors. You don't even know why your eyes are like that in the first place! Why should you get all the attention while I'm being thrown under the bus?" He started to pace around the room mumbling to himself.

"Is this really what all of this is about?" I questioned in my head. I never asked to be famous, and I wouldn't even consider this "being famous." I never wanted to be this way.

The doctor stopped mumbling and turned to me. "Don't worry about your fame right now," he started, "because your eyes will no longer be a problem when I'm done getting rid of one of them."

I was losing it, trying to move, but it was no use. He had to be insane! Why would you take out someone else's eye, was he crazy? The nurse sat quietly on the other side of the room. Then the doctor gave her some sort of signal and she nodded. She walked over to a tray, taking out a large needle filled with something tapenade colored. The doctor took the needle out of her hand, walked over to me, and pointed it at my head.

"Sorry, but I have to do this," he said. He then raised his hand in the air, and with a very quick motion, slammed the needle down into my forehead.

∽

I could move around and was standing in a very dark room. I couldn't really see anything but I was no longer in pain, which was relieving. Things started to become a little bit clearer, so I waited until I could completely see. Once things cleared up, I looked around so I could see where I was. Looking around, I saw that I was in a hospital room. On the hospital bed I could see a girl with black hair and light-blue colored skin being operated on. She had scars all over her, and needles stuck everywhere. It took me a moment to realize it, but suddenly I understood that the girl on the table was me! How could I be standing on the opposite side of the room if I was also over there? That didn't make any sense. Why couldn't the doctor or the nurse see me?

Then, abruptly, things got cold. I could feel a hand slowly resting on my shoulder. I turned around to see who was touching me, and I almost started screaming. The shadow that had been trying to kill me all this time, that we had finally managed to kill, was right next to me. I stood still waiting for it to attack me, but it did nothing. I looked at it, confused, and it gave me a look.

"Are you finished freaking out?" it asked me. I quietly nodded. "You're probably confused because you're in two places at once right?"

"Can you explain that to me please?" I asked.

"I'm surprised you haven't figured out that you can do this earlier. Your parents should have told you this, but it's too late for that now, isn't it?" it asked jokingly.

I looked at it with an annoyed look.

"Anyways," it continued, "remember all those people telling you that your eyes are special?"

"Yes, what's so special about heterochromia?" I asked.

"You don't have heterochromia. You're not even human."

I looked at it like it was crazy. Of course I'm human. Both of my parents are human, so why wouldn't I be?

"Before you were born, your parents never wanted a child at all. There were also two shadows who wanted their own children at the time, but it's impossible for shadows to have children of their own unless they are in possession of a human body. They decided to possess the bodies of your parents. When it was time for you to be birthed, they didn't want the doctors to find out that the parents were possessed so they left once you were born. You were born with two different eyes Jani, a green one and a colorless one. Shadows have no color in their eyes, so which eye do you think is the real one?" it asked.

I had to process all the information given to me. So, my parents aren't my actual parents? I would be classified as a shadow?

"My real eye is the colorless one, right?"

The shadow nodded. "Your other eye is green because you were born from human parents."

"If my parents never wanted any children, why did they take care of me when

I was younger?" I asked, hoping everything that was said was false, but as always, there's an answer.

"When you were younger, you weren't aware of your surroundings. Your parents were possessed at the time. Once the humans your parents possessed found out, they tried to kill you."

"This doesn't really explain why I'm here right now, why is there two of me, and how are you here I thought we killed you?" I asked wanting answers.

"The reason I am still here is the same reason you're in two places at once," it explained. "All shadows have the ability to be in more than one place at once. You didn't kill me, you killed another part of me, but you didn't kill the main vessel."

Everything started to make sense. The one laying in the hospital bed wasn't the real me, so taking that eye would be meaningless.

"Jani, I might need to warn you, though."

I turned to look at the shadow, it had a serious look on its face.

"I want you to listen very closely. Even though you are part shadow, you are still part human, which is holding you back from the real you."

The real me? What was it talking about?

"Jani, the real you is hidden in that colorless eye of yours. Whenever you come face to face with something you can't handle, don't try to fight back, because the other you will take over, understood?"

I nodded, surprised.

"Try not to get angry either, just being angry can trigger the inner you."

We stood there for a while in silence.

The shadow then turned to me and said, "You better get going. The doctor can't see you now, but once the other you in the hospital bed wakes up, you're visible to everyone."

"What happens when it wakes up?" I asked.

"It will evaporate immediately. Now hurry, you don't have that much time."

I walked into the hallway, where the light is dimmed down. Once I made it to the room that Shafty, Daniel, and Liam were in, I tried to reach for the doorknob, but my hand slid right through. I tried to just walk through the door, and it worked just fine. In the room you could see Daniel and Shafty playing cards, while Liam was asleep in the corner. They seemed to be just fine, so I went back into the hallway and decided to see the other patients that were there.

I walked into one room where I saw a woman who seemed to be paralyzed. In another room I could see a man watching the small television provided. In another room there was a small little boy crying in pain, while his mother was next to him trying to calm him down. Seeing this made me angry. The doctor had so many patients, but only cared about his fame. I walked away extremely frustrated, with no clue where I was going.

The hallway came to a stop at a small door. I walked inside without any thought. "What am I doing? Why am I going in here?" I thought to myself. In the room there was a small shelf. The shelf had a small box cutter on it, and I picked it up. I walked out of the room, seething with pure rage. Who did that doctor think he was, torturing these innocent people just to gain attention? I walked towards the room that the other me came from. Once I got inside, I saw the doctor make the other me drink something. On a tray I could see two eyes in jars. When the other me drank the drink, it awoke immediately and disappeared, along with the two eyes in the jars. The doctor looked surprised and confused, while the nurse ran out of the room. When the doctor turned around, he saw me and looked terrified. I couldn't think straight, and I stared right at the doctor.

As if on cue, I couldn't control myself at all. I charged right at him. Everything was blurry then—all I could see was red. Then, I seemed to flash forward. I looked down to see the doctor crying and begging me to stop. He had cuts and blood all over him. I looked in my hand and saw the box cutter covered in blood. This might seem wrong, but whatever I did calmed me down a lot. Without thinking, I grabbed the doctor by the collar and started talking to him in a language that I couldn't even understand. It's like something was controlling my body. That's when I remembered the talk the shadow had with me about the inner me inside that would come out when I was angry. Even so, I felt calmer than usual. Is that wrong? I walked over to a tray and grabbed a bundle of needles. I walked to the hallway, into a broom closet, where the nurse from before was hiding. My vision then went blurry again, and when things cleared up, the nurse was on the ground with needles stuck on her everywhere. I didn't understand this feeling. It seemed so calming, but it shouldn't be. I was murdering people, and this is a serious crime! Yet, I didn't feel any remorse for my actions.

I turned around to see the shadow that visited me earlier standing there.

"Remember when I told you not to get angry" it asked.

I nodded then realized what it was talking about. I wasn't in control of my own body, it was the real me taking control.

"Why didn't I feel remorseful afterwards?" I asked.

"You weren't able to control your actions, right? It's the same thing—you couldn't control your emotions either," it explained, walking over to the nurse and scrutinizing her wounds.

"Is there any way I can get rid of her?" I asked.

"You only have two options to choose from Jani: either we get of her, or we could separate the two of you from one another."

"Why would I want to do that? Wouldn't she kill us all?"

If we separate, then I feared there was a possibility she would go on a murderous rampage, and I might become a victim.

The shadow looked at me with a smile and said "Jani, I was watching the entire murder scene with you two happen. I'm not entirely sure, but I think she's already on your side to begin with. After seeing the poor hospital people and whatever Dr. Slaughter did to you, it made her angry and it seems like the only way she expresses anger is death."

That made a lot more sense. She never tried to hurt me at all, and the only reason we killed the doctor and nurse was because of their actions.

"How do we separate from each other?" I asked.

"A wise decision, but doing that is beyond my abilities. I know someone who could help you with your situation."

CHAPTER TWELVE
TWO OF ME

WE WALKED BACK to the room where the others were.

"Won't they be able to see you?" I asked the shadow who was following me.

"Nope, only you can see me right now. I'm sure they would freak out if they saw me."

I nodded as I headed toward the door. Opening it, I walked in toward the group. Once they saw me their faces all lit up with excitement, and then, a look of confusion.

"I'm so glad you're ok, but where did the doctor go?" Daniel asked.

I was afraid that they would ask that question.

"The doctor wasn't trying to help me, he tried to steal one of my eyes."

The others looked surprised.

"Where is he now?" Shafty asked.

Before I could say anything, the shadow whispered in my ear, "Don't tell them you killed him, and don't even tell them our plan."

I had to think of a lie quickly.

"The doctor left, but he asked for you guys to take care of the residents that are here, I have to go and run some errands elsewhere," I lied, hoping that they would believe it.

They seemed to believe it and they all stood up.

Liam groaned and said, "Do we have to?"

Shafty punched his arm, giving him a glare.

"What errands are you tending to Jani?" Daniel asked, ignoring the other two.

"It's a simple task, I'm not sure how long I'll be gone though," I said with a smile. I left the room and made my way out of the hospital.

It was dark, cold, and raining outside—my least favorite kind of weather. The shadow led me to this dark, small, and creepy looking shop. It was far away from the other buildings in Shadows Creek. Dead trees surrounded the shop and it smelled of freshly cut grass.

"Is this place safe?" I asked the shadow, worried.

"Of course it is, you'll be surprised once you go inside" the shadow said, smiling.

We walked inside of the small shop and once we got in, I immediately loved this place. It was humongous on the inside, so much bigger than on the outside. There were lanterns and other lights filling the room. The entire place smelled like a bakery. It has a steampunk-style feel to it.

"This place is amazing!" I said.

The shadow just smiled, and I followed her to the front desk, where a man stood. He wore a large top hat with random gadgets on it, and he held a scepter in his hand. He turned to look at us and smiled.

"Hello, what can I do for you?" he asked. He had a slight British accent in his voice.

"Ophidian, I need your help with something" the shadow said with a serious face.

The man, whose name must be Ophidian, looked puzzled and asked, "What do you need help with?"

"I need you to use your disembody treatment on my friend Jani, here."

His face lit up and he looked at me. He walked closer and looked at my face. While looking at him I saw that his eyes look just like a snake's. Without warning, he jumped up in excitement, and I watched him, confused.

"She's just like me, isn't she?" Ophidian asked the shadow.

"In a way she is," the shadow said.

He looked at me and pointed to his eyes. "I'm possessed by the snake spirit named Apep. Just like you are possessed by the shadow that is in your eye." While he talked, I saw something slither from behind him. It slowly slithered up to his shoulder and rested its head. It was an albino King Snake, but something about it seemed oddly weird. He looked at it and laughed. "This is the snake that possessed my body. I disembodied him and now he's pretty much my best friend."

The shadow looked at me and said, "this is what we are going to be doing to you Jani." I looked at Ophidian and his snake and just nodded. I had high hopes this would turn out well, but knew with my extreme bad luck, it probably wouldn't.

Ophidian led us into a room in the back of the shop and let us inside. The room was dark and had a few blue-colored lights inside. He walked me over to a table and I sat, watching him work. The shadow took a seat farther away from me. All of my confidence suddenly disappeared and I was terrified. Ophidian grabbed a weird looking object that looked like a torch. He whispered something to the torch, I couldn't quite make out what he said, but I waited for him to finish. As soon as he stopped whispering, the torch lit up on fire. The fire didn't look like a normal fire though, because the flames were blue. He looked dead at me and yelled something that I couldn't understand.

"Έχετε για τη δική σας φόρμα του θανάτου για το σχήμα
που θα διαχωριστεί από το ανθρώπινο πνεύμα!"

All of a sudden, a blast of blinding light headed toward me. Before I could move anywhere, the light hit me with a force that felt like being pushed over in a wave.

When the light vanished, I opened my eyes and saw someone else in front of me, passed out on the ground. She looked exactly like me, except the color of the scarf and sweater were switched. She slowly opened her eyes and looked at me. Instead of having one green eye, her eye was red. As she stood up and stared at me, she said, "Don't be scared, I'm not like the others I won't hurt you!"

This was the most uneasy thing to process. I was talking to myself, literally, and it was hard to handle.

"What do you mean when you say you're not like the others?" I asked her.

"I'm not like the other shadows you've fought against Jani." She explained to me.

"How do you know about that?" I asked, wondering how she knew about the fight between the shadows.

"You should at least know by now that I've been with you this entire time, even when you were born. I know it may sound creepy, but I had no choice since I was stuck in your eye all the time," she said, giving me a small smile.

"This is so weird, it's almost like she's talking in a mirror." Ophidian said.

"It might be a little bit difficult to get used to, but I'm sure that we all can handle this," the strange copy explained.

All of us agree and we are ready to leave Ophidian's shop. "Come back to my shop anytime Jani!" he called out as we left.

We walked towards Dr. Slaughter's hospital to pick up Shafty, Daniel, and Liam. "Wait, what are we going to tell the others when we get back?" I asked, motioning towards the other me. "If they see me with her, they'll go crazy."

Instead of the shadow answering the other me stepped in. "Don't worry about it, if you've already forgotten, I'm a shadow too, so they won't be able to see me, only you will."

"All you need to do is make sure you don't slip out and tell them what happened recently today accidently," the shadow told me.

On the way there I had a question in mind that I had to ask the shadowed me. "What do you want me to call you?" I asked her.

She thought for a while and responded, "If it makes you feel better, you can just call me J if you want to." I nodded. Calling her J was way better than just calling her 'the other me.'

We made it to the hospital, and inside I saw Shafty, Daniel and Liam helping all the other mistreated patients. Liam ran up to me and said, "We treated some of the patients, but all of them said that they've been here for a very long time, and that the doctor never came to help them."

Shafty came over to speak as well. "Hey what happened while you were gone?"

"Nothing much I just went for a long walk somewhere," I said, obviously lying.

"What about the errand you had to do?" Daniel asked, joining the conversation.

"I just had to take something out," I said lying again. "Are all of the patients treated and taken out of here?" I asked, changing the subject so they wouldn't get suspicious.

"There is one patient left in one of the rooms, but I think you need to see what's going on with him, because I think it's something we should probably worry about," Shafty told me, with a slightly worried face.

She walked me down to the room where the last patient was. Once we got there, we walked inside, and on the hospital bed there was a young boy sitting there and staring at the wall. He was blue like everyone else and had very messy hair. He looked around seven years old. The lights were off and the room was really dark, except for a few candles in the.

"He's been staring at the wall for the past 5 hours," Shafty whispered to me.

"Hello there I'm back." Shafty said to the child.

"*Hello...*" the kid responded with a raspy voice, still staring at the wall. There was something seriously off with this kid. Why was he staring at the wall, I speculated.

"Are you feeling alright?" I asked him, feeling a bit worried and afraid.

Suddenly the kid perked up, and looked at me. He didn't say anything, but just sat there and stared right at me. I was little surprised by his sudden boost of energy, and kind of scared by the way he was looking at me. The young boy looked like he had just seen a ghost. He didn't say anything for a while, and then, "Are you Jani Topia?" he asked, not taking his eyes of me.

"Why do you want to know that?" Shafty said, questioning the child. He ignored Shafty and looked at me with inquisitive eyes. "Say no..." Shafty whispered to me.

"No I'm not Jani, I'm not entirely sure who that might be," I lied to the little boy. His face changed to sudden anger.

"You're lying to me, aren't you? I know you are because the ghost lady told me so!" he said with a slight rage in his voice. What ghost lady was this little boy talking about? I surely hoped it wasn't another problem I had to deal with because I've always been terrified of ghosts.

"What ghost lady are you talking about?" Shafty asked. The boy ignored her once again, which left Shafty irritated and she left the room, slamming the door. She left me alone with the kid in the dark.

"Why won't you talk to Shafty?" I asked the boy carefully.

"I don't like her, she seems shady," he said. I thought it was funny, because that's what I thought of Shafty when I first met her.

"Don't worry, you can trust her," I told him. "So, can you at least tell me who the ghost lady is?"

He paused for a moment and stared at the wall. He then turned back and said, "she doesn't want me to tell you who she is." That meant that this ghost lady the boy was talking about was in the hospital, and messing with this young boy.

"You can see the ghost, right?" I asked the boy quietly. He looked at me and nodded. "How many ghosts do you see here?"

"There's too many here to count," he said.

Then the candles went out and it was pitch black.

CHAPTER THIRTEEN
ANOTHER PROBLEM TO DEAL WITH

I HAD REACHED my breaking point and started screaming for help. Ghosts are my number one fear, and I couldn't handle this situation well. I tried to look for the door, but I couldn't see anything. A hand grabbed my scarf and tugged on it gently, and I started freaking out even more. One candle had been lit in one corner of the room. I saw that the little boy had left the hospital bed and was now holding the corner of my scarf in his hands. I slowly took the scarf away from him.

"The ghost lady told me to tell you that you shouldn't run," the little boy said.

"Who exactly is the ghost lady?" I asked him, still reaching for a door.

"She won't tell me her name, she said it's not important."

"Can you at least tell me what the lady looks like?"

He looked over at the candle in the corner of the room, not saying anything, then looked back at me.

"She's really tall and has very pretty black eyes," he said. "I don't like her bloody hands, though, that's scary."

On the other side of the door there was knocking and yelling, and I tried to open it, but couldn't. The little boy walked over to the candle and blew it out. Everything became black again, so I couldn't see anymore. The others were finally able to make it in the room and turned on the lights. Just as I thought that the ghost would hurt me, the others had finally opened the door.

"What happened in here?" Shafty asked.

I didn't respond though, because the boy was back on the hospital bed and looking at the wall like nothing happened. He slowly glared at me then went back to looking at the wall. There was something wrong with the wall, I assumed, if he stared at it constantly, but I just couldn't figure it out. The others stood there waiting for an answer, but I didn't say anything, and walked toward the kid. He looked at me like he was worried about something. I whispered in his ear as quietly as I possibly could, so nobody else could hear.

"Can you please point to where the ghost is?"

He didn't do anything for a while, and the others looked confused, but I stood there and waited for him to do something. He lifted his hand and pointed to the candles in the corner. Then he pointed to another candle in the room, and he went on to point to each candle in the room.

The lights in the room started to rumble and break, making the room dark again. The candles began to light up and blow out over and over without stopping. One of the candles fell off of a table and broke, causing another candle to light up even more. Each candle broke, one after the next. Whenever one broke, another one got bigger, until it reached the corner candle. The flame was dangerously large and terrifying. The boy next to me started sobbing very loudly, and the candle started to flame up even more. The boy started screaming at this point, and I didn't know what to do.

"What's going on kid?!" I yelled.

The ground started shaking vigorously.

"It's all your fault! You made the ghost angry at me and now it's going to kill me!" he screamed at me.

I looked at the candle, while trying to keep my balance and not fall. A burst of flames flew across the room, and the room became so hot I could barely breathe. An ear piercing shriek filled the room and everyone had to cover their ears.

All at once, the room seemed to be cooling down and no one was injured, which was a relief. However, the kid wasn't in the bed anymore. The bed had black ashes on it, and there was smoke filling the room. It smelled like burnt tires in here, which was disgusting, by the way.

"Where'd the kid go?" Liam asked me. I just shrugged my shoulders because I was absolutely speechless.

After I regained my thoughts, I left the room to search for the kid and past the others to the front of the hospital. I looked outside the window and saw a gigantic flame. The flame slowly cooled down, into black smoke. Two piercing, white eyes were the only thing you could see. I've seen those eyes before, and I wish it wasn't what I thought it was, but sadly it was true. This entire time I thought we had been rid of the shadows, but apparently we didn't do anything if they're sitting right here in front of me. I couldn't understand how the shadows could be back. Didn't we destroy them?

Behind me the shadow that I was with said, "Remember how I told you I never really died? The same goes with all shadows."

In a separate room, I found the little boy standing next to the shadow and noticed me looking through the window.

"You can see her too, right?" he said. "This is the ghost lady I was talking to you about. She told me that she has been looking for you everywhere and that she has been waiting forever to meet you again."

I looked back at the shadow behind me. "How are we supposed to get rid of them then and why didn't you tell me this earlier?" I asked it. "I thought they would have left you guys alone by now, but I guess they still haven't forgotten about you."

The shadows outside glanced over at us, and their eyes opened wide then filled with rage. It pointed at the shadow behind me and screeched loudly.

"TRAITOR!" it yelled.

"YOU'RE THE TRAITOR!" the shadow behind me screamed back.

It's the loudest I've ever heard it yell before. The two shadows started to argue with each other back and forth ignoring me and the young boy. I walk out of the hospital quietly and crouched down next to the little kid.

"Do you like being with her?" I asked him, pointing to the shadow in front of us." He glanced without saying anything, like he was afraid to answer. He didn't say anything, but he did shake his head no slightly. "Would you like to come with me instead?" I asked him.

"You seem like a very nice person Jani, but I don't really know you, so how would I be able to trust you?" he whispered.

I thought for a little while. There had to be a way to make this small boy trust me, because I didn't want to leave him here with the shadow. There was a big chance that the shadow might try to kill this kid, and I didn't want it to happen, nor would I let it.

I looked the kid right in the eyes and said, "I know you don't fully trust me yet, but you at least have to know that I am most certainly not like this psychopath that you are going everywhere with. The ghost lady that you might think is a good person is a murderer, and I will do the best I can to save you from her. So please, I beg of you, come with me."

The kid stared at me with large eyes. I held out my hand to help him up. He hesitated for a moment, and then grabbed my hand. I helped him back to his feet and looked at the other two shadows. They were still arguing with each other, but this time in a different language so the boy and I wouldn't be able to understand. I slowly walked the boy towards the entrance of the hospital, but I stopped when I heard the shadow scream angrily. Apparently, she noticed that the boy and I managed to escape.

Instantly a huge force pulled us back, away from the door. My eyes started to burn, and it was hard to breathe. All I could see was black smoke again. I tried struggling to move but the force that pulled me away suddenly closed tighter, crushing me within it. It let go, then, and I started falling. My heart dropped. I felt my leg get caught, and suddenly was dangling. The shadow must have dropped me. My eyes started to cool down a bit, and when I opened them, I saw that we were at least fifty yards away from the ground. Next to me, the little boy was also looking at the ground below us. He didn't say anything, he just watched. I looked at him for a while and decided not to panic too much. I realized I should take this situation and think about it rationally, instead of going crazy or panicking too much. I watched the ground below us as well, while thinking. Where was this shadow taking us anyway? Was she taking me because I tried to take the little boy with me, or did she find out about what happened to my father? Both were possible reasons, and, as a matter of fact, the shadow's anger could be fueled by both possibilities.

I never really noticed how large Shadows Creek is. It's kind of beautiful in its own little way. The boy beside me was still as quiet as ever, so I decided that I should at least say something to him.

"Does the shadow always carry you like this?" I asked him, trying to engage him in a conversation.

"Yes, all of the time. I don't like it, though. It burns when she grabs me," he said, still looking down.

Poor kid, he's had to go through a lot if this is happening to him. "Where are your mother and father? They must be worried sick about you," I asked him.

He didn't say anything for a while. "I don't have parents anymore, because my parents are both dead. The shadows killed them." He looked at me and his eyes were starting to fill up with tears. "I don't want to talk about it, you don't understand what I'm going through. Nobody does."

He's just like me, then, because I lost both of my parents. As a matter of fact, I lost both twice. "I do know what you are going through. Both of my parents are deceased as well. They both faked their death at first, then later, they died," I said, unenthusiastically.

His eyes widened, "Your parents must be terrible people," he said. I didn't have the heart to tell him that my family were the people who created the shadows... Or the fact that the real me is a shadow and I'm just a copy. It would probably have scared him half to death, which is something I was trying hard to avoid. I didn't want anyone else to suffer because of me or my family problems.

Very slowly, the shadow dropped down to the ground, letting us go. It let us go before we made it to the ground and both of us hit the ground hard, which really hurt.

"Where are you taking us?" I asked.

"I don't have to tell you, now shut your mouth!"

I quickly glanced away without saying anything else. We were led into a very dark looking cave. No light came in nor out of the subterranean area. We walked in and once we got inside, I couldn't see anything. This wasn't really where I expected the shadow to take us at all, but I shouldn't judge so quickly. A tiny spark was illuminated in the middle of the cave, which slowly turned into a small fire on a pile of trash and sticks from outside. The fire lit up the room and the second I looked around, I started to get lightheaded. The entire group of shadows was in the cave.

Some were tall, some were short, and some seemed very faint, making it hard to see what their features.

"What's going on here?" I asked the small boy quietly. Before the kid could answer, one of the shadows in the back spoke.

"We are the remaining shadows that survived from the big fight you had with the other shadows," it explained. "The only shadows that you were able to kill were the extremely weak ones, but we are the ones that either you couldn't kill or escaped before you could even try."

Another shadow that was closer to me spoke up. "We have recently learned that you yourself are indeed a shadow. So, we are all here today to inform you that you're joining us."

They could not be serious. I tried to kill them all, and now they wanted me to join them?

"What are you talking about? I would never join your stupid group of murderers!" I yelled.

The shadow that dragged me here started talking. "I don't know if you noticed but you really don't have a choice. Your family comes from a group of murderers and you *are* part shadow."

"I hate to break it to you, but I am no longer part shadow anymore because I got it separated into its own living form! Also, for your information, I *do* have a choice."

Every shadow in the room looked genuinely surprised at what I said, which made me a little confused.

"There's a separate shadow version of you out there, and it's the original you?"

one of the shadows asked. I nodded, still as confused as ever, while the boy next to me looked at me with wide eyes. Every shadow in the room left in a large and quick hurry making the fire burn out.

The cavern was dark again and one of the shadows yelled back, "We don't need you two anymore!"

I walked slowly trying to make my way out of the cave. Once I got there, I saw the little boy standing there and watching me. "You're not an evil person are you?" he asked. "The shadows said that you were born in a family of murderers, is that true?"

I didn't want to lie to this kid. "Yes I was born into an evil family, but I myself am not an evil person I can promise you that," I told him just to reassure him. Then I realized what was happening. The shadows were going to look for J, just so they could get her to join them all because she's a shadow. I was sure she wouldn't say yes, and she also was able to hide herself from others. The only problem was the fact that I didn't know if she could hide herself from other shadows considering she was one herself.

CHAPTER FOURTEEN
THE RESCUE MISSION

I THOUGHT TO myself about the fact that the shadows had probably made it to the hospital and caught J already. I should have been going to help her, but wondered what I could even do without a plan, or anything, or anyone to help me?

Across from me the little boy sat on the ground not saying anything. He really was a very quiet kid. I sat down next to him and I tried to think of some type of plan that could stop my terrible fate, but my mind kept drifting. Why couldn't everything in life be normal for once in a while? Why couldn't I finally get rid of everything and just restart? Why was I the victim out of all people? My parents were liars, and not even my real parents. I turned out to be one of the most feared beings in Shadows Creek, and I wasn't even the original version of myself! For a while I sat and thought about everything that happened to me since I came to Shadows Creek.

Just then I realized something. There was

someone who could help us with this situation, someone who was great with magic, and had a lot of knowledge about shadows.

"Hey, I know where we can go," I told the little boy who was sitting by me. He just nodded and stood up with me. Then I remembered that I had no Idea where we were, so I had no choice but to walk around for a while.

"You don't know where we are, do you?" the kid asked, bluntly.

"I've never been to this place before, so I don't really know my way around this area," I said, shrugging my shoulders.

"Where are you trying to go?" he asked.

"Do you know where Ophidian's magic shop is?" I asked him, expecting a no, but apparently, I was wrong.

"You could have just asked me—I know where his shop is. It's not too far from here, we can get there quickly," he said with a smile. Then he led me around the woods, taking us to the magic shop. Ophidian would surely help us. He helped me with my shadow problems, so he'd probably help us with this.

Once we got there, I saw that it was the exact same as it was before: an abandoned building on the outside, though once we were inside I was sure it would be as astonishing as it was the last I came here. Inside the building I could see all the lights that were here last time are now shut off, and around the room were very small lamps, making a dim light around the room. It was just enough light to barely see.

As I walked around the room, I tried my best not to knock down anything valuable. The little boy slowly followed behind me, also trying to avoid knocking anything over. In the far back of the room, sitting in a recliner, was Ophidian, fast asleep with his hat still on his head, and his pet snake who has taken control over a part of Ophidian's body on his shoulder. The snake was kind of amusing to look at, in a way. I didn't really know how to wake Ophidian up from his slumber, and I didn't really want to disturb him. I understood that asking him to do this might be too much, considering the other favor that he'd done for me... But, this was the only viable choice to make—the other options most certainly leading to death.

"Are you just going to stand there?" Ophidian said, one of his eyes opening and a smile on his face. "Or are you going to tell me about the entire swarm of shadows that went by not so long ago?"

"About that... the shadows kidnapped us and now they're on their way to find J, the shadow version of me. So, we came here to see if you would help us... so would you please help us with this issue?" I asked him, sort of nervously.

He looked at us for a while and started to laugh, which was confusing.

"What's so funny?" the little boy asked Ophidian with an irritated look on his face.

"It's funny because you didn't need to come here. I've already started helping you with your little problem. The hospital is currently invisible to the shadows who are searching for your shadow friend."

I stood there dumb-founded. How did he know anything about the shadows? He wasn't even there at the time.

"How did you find out about the shadows Ophidian?" the boy questioned. He was probably just as confused as I was.

"Did you two really forget that I live and work in a hidden magic shop?" he laughed, with a smirk. The snake on his shoulder woke from his sleep and made his way right over to me. It slithered its way to my arm and wrapped itself around it. "Keep him with you Jani, I'm not allowed to leave the shop, but he can. Take him and he will show you what to do.

"Why can't you leave the shop Ophidian?" I asked while petting the snake on my arm.

"I wish I could tell you Jani, but that's a secret I have to keep for myself," he replied with a disappointed look on his face.

The little boy and I left the shop to find our way to the hospital. While we walked, the dead leaves crinkled and the small twigs snapped as we stepped on them, which was annoyingly loud. We stopped somewhere in the middle of the woods. Around there we could hear two people talking. The snake wrapped around my arm slithered its way far away from us. We didn't know where it went, so we just stayed where we were for a while. The two voices started to get louder, and we could hear someone heading our way. The small boy held on to me while I had a slight panic attack. In the distance we could see two dark figures heading our way at full speed. A large, deafening explosion could be heard, and a blinding, blue light shone from the area where the two dark figures were.

The snake came back, and with Ophidian's voice said, "I merely stunned them for a while, but they'll be back if we don't leave fast enough."

It slithered up my arm again, and the little boy and I started running while Ophidian gave us directions. In the far distance we could hear blood curdling screams coming from multiple people. It sounded like it was Liam, Daniel, and

Shafty. I hoped the shadows hadn't gotten them yet. I started running faster, praying the little boy could catch up. Turns out the little boy was just as fast. We both made our way to the hospital to find that there was nothing there.

"Keep walking, put your arms up as well," Ophidian said.

I did what he said and walked forward. After a few yards of walking, I felt a hard, wood surface. I felt it for a while, finding a door knob, turning it, and discovering the hospital on the other side. We both walked in, and I make sure to close the door behind me. Inside I could see the shadow me, J, and Shafty playing cards. Daniel and the shadow were just talking to each other, and Liam was just being himself. I walked over to them with a confused face.

"Don't worry," Daniel said, "they told us everything, and I understand that you didn't want us being worried."

"You still could've told us at least *something* so we wouldn't worry about you," Shafty said, still playing cards.

"I'm so sorry you guys I didn't want you to worry about me," I said, apologizing.

"Don't worry about it," Daniel said.

"Where did you even go?" J asked.

"About that… there's an entire swarm of shadows on their way here," I confessed.

"Why are they coming here?" the shadow asked.

"They thought that we were useless, so now they're coming after J, and we're lucky that we got here before them." J didn't say anything, she just sat there quietly.

Liam stood up and walked over to me, pointing at Ophidian's snake. "Why is there a snake around your arm Jani?" he asked, ignoring the whole situation.

"This is the snake that belongs to Ophidian, the person who helped separate J from me."

Liam reached out to touch the snake when he was interrupted by Ophidian's voice. "Do not touch the snake please, he has delicate scales, and gets angered when anyone pets him."

Liam, being startled by the voice, stepped back away from the snake. "I wasn't expecting you to talk at all," Liam exclaimed.

"I do talk, but I would please like to get back at the task at hand."

The shadow walked up to Ophidian and asked, "Do you know how to get rid of the shadows, Ophidian?"

Shafty suddenly had the most confused face ever. "Wait a second, if you're a shadow, shouldn't you know how to get rid of pretty much yourself?"

The shadow gave a slightly nervous chuckle and said, "I may be a shadow, but I don't know how to kill my own kind."

Ophidian explained, "There is only one way to get rid of them, but it's very dangerous, and could possibly get us injured."

J finally decided to speak, but her voice was weak and nervous. "Jani, you don't plan to get rid of us, do you? I mean, we are shadows too."

I looked at the two of them and shook my head no. I didn't want to get rid of the shadow or J, because the two of them never did anything to me. I mean, the shadow *did* try to kill me once, but it changed *a lot*. The shadow was much nicer and didn't have the urge to kill me anymore.

The snake slithered to the middle of the room and said, "I can get rid of the shadows, but I will need the help of you seven. I do not want to be let down. I'll tell you the plan once the shadows make their way, I'll only walk you through the plan during the battle, understand?" We all agreed with him, oblivious to the actual plan.

"What are we supposed to do now?" Liam asked, with a bored look on his face.

"Now we just wait for our visitors to arrive, and then I'll tell you what to do." Ophidian explained.

"What do we do until then?" Liam complained.

"I could care less about what you do, as long as you absolutely do not leave the building. The hospital isn't visible to the other shadows out there, but we're all visible to them. It could take them a while to make their way over here."

CHAPTER FIFTEEN

A TRAITOR AND A FORCED ROOMMATE

WE WERE ALL together playing cards, waiting for something to happen, until a something hit the building with a large thud. We also heard a loud screech. The thuds seemed to hit all sides of the building.

"What are we supposed to do now?" Daniel asked, yelling over the noise. The ground started shaking vigorously.

The snake responded quickly, and with warning. "Whatever happens here, do not think differently of Jani. What I need you to do is hide somewhere safely outside of the hospital, and keep J and the other shadow safe. They both are not allowed to look at what happens, or else they both will die because they're both shadows." The snake then turned to me and said, "You're going to stay with me, understand?"

I just nodded in return, confused about what is happening here. The rest of the group snuck out the back of the hospital while I stayed where I was. The snake slithered back up my arm holding on so tightly, it was sort of painful.

"Jani, whatever happens, do not become afraid," he said, and then continued to lay out the plan. "I'm going to need you to get the shadows attention and lure them back into the building. I'll handle the rest from there."

I didn't really know how to distract them. So, I just started to walk out of the hospital without saying anything. The swarms of shadows stopped moving, and I saw a large number of eyes looking right back at me.

"How did you get here *before* us?!" a booming voice screamed.

"You're really getting on my nerves and I want you *dead*!" another voice screeched.

The shadows started running toward me at full speed without stopping. It looked like a giant, dark cloud growing larger and larger. I ran as fast as I could back inside.

I looked back and could hear Ophidian yell, "Brace yourself! This might hurt a bit!"

A blinding white light filled the room, it turned red, and then, pitch black. I could hardly breathe at all. Suddenly the discolored eye started to itch, but I couldn't move. It started to burn, but became excruciating pain. Finally the pain hurt so much I couldn't take it. I started to scream, but no sound came out at all. I couldn't deal with it anymore. I wanted all of this to be over with. Ophidian said that it would hurt, but he never said that it would hurt this much. I tried my best to move even one muscle, but it was useless.

The pain started to cool down and the blackness began to fade back into a scenery of black splotches everywhere. The hospital was absolutely destroyed. The walls were shattered, and the ceiling had crashed. I put my hand on my forehead, something must have hit it, because it was bleeding. My arms had freshly cut wounds in them. The snake that was on my arm wasn't there anymore, it was now clinging to one of my legs, which also had small bruises.

I looked over to see Shafty, Daniel, Liam, and the others running toward me. Before they could say anything, they just stood there, shocked and staring at me. Before I could say anything, Shafty reached down to the ground and picked up one of the broken pieces of mirrors off the ground and showed it to me. I almost threw up—not from panic, fear, or disgust— but from being overly excited about the reflection in the mirror. I had one eye that was green and another eye that was the exact same color.

I smiled in the mirror until Liam said, "I didn't even know your eye could do something like that, Jani." I looked at him confused, then look at the others who looked just as eager to hear my answer.

"Don't tell me that you don't know what just happened." Daniel said with a puzzled look on his face.

"What happened?" I asked them curiously.

Shafty explained everything that happened for me. "The shadows made the building crash and you ended up getting really hurt because a large chunk of the ceiling hit your head. But you got up like nothing happened and you started screaming. A blast of red light escaped from your eye which blasted the shadows. We were scared at first, until we saw the shadows dropping one by one. Whenever one tried to escape, it didn't work out for them, because they still got hit. After all of the shadows died, you just dropped to the ground."

Shafty said it so quickly I had to take the time to process all of that. I looked at the black splotches on the ground. I couldn't believe I did all that. I looked at the snake who was on my leg. It loosened up and slithered away, fast. It assumed it went back to Ophidian's shop. The others watched him slither away as well.

"We should go back to Ophidian's shop and thank him." I say.

On the way to Ophidian's shop, we saw the people of Shadows Creek all cheering for someone. They were all laughing and celebrating around something. As some of the crowd cleared, we could get a slight glimpse of who the crowd was gathering around. We saw Ophidian smiling and talking with people. He was shaking hands and taking pictures with others, wearing an unsettling grin on his face. Shafty suddenly ran over to him very angrily without saying anything to us.

"He's taking all the credit," J said with an irritated voice.

"Sure, he was a great help," I said. "He helped Jani and I split into two, he helped us with our shadow problem, he helped tremendously, but he can't take *all* of the credit."

"Jani and the little boy literally almost died, and when the people of the hospital were in grave danger, we were the ones who tended to their emergencies," Liam added.

We ran as fast as we could to keep up with Shafty who didn't stop moving.

"…It was tough but I managed, I even had this group of children try to stop me from doing my job. They even harassed me just so I could help them with their needs," Ophidian said, lying. "I went through so much pain, both of my parents died and tried to kill me. I then realized that they never loved me at all and I'm heartbroken. How could they do such a thing?"

That was *me* who went through all of that pain, I thought to myself. *I* had to watch my father get torn apart, and it was my own mother and father who both tried to murder *me*! He walked away from the crowd and walked toward two sturdy looking guards dressed in blue uniforms with a badges that said "Prison Guards" on them.

"The only reason we're letting you off house arrest is because everyone here thinks you're some type of hero," said the guard.

"But I believe otherwise," interjected the other guard, "considering your criminal record."

Ophidian looked at the guards with a glare.

"Can you at least arrest those children, considering what they did to me?"

Shafty walked up to one of the guards before he could answer and whispered something in his ear. The guard nodded and whispered to the other guard with a serious face. The guard marched up to Ophidian and put him back in handcuffs.

"What are you doing? You let me go, you can't put me in handcuffs—I saved everyone in this town!" Shafty walked over to him and punched him in the face.

"You're just going to let her do that?" Ophidian asked the guard as if Shafty didn't even touch him.

"I'll allow it," the guard said smiling.

"Why did you betray us?" the little boy asked, who had been quiet for a while. Ophidian didn't say anything, he just glared at the boy and looked at the guard.

"How can you even trust them? They don't have any proof that they helped at all. You can't arrest me unless you have full evidence that they did something."

The two guards looked at each other with puzzled faces. One of the guards sighed and glanced at us with a depressing look. "We have to put you all in hand-cuffs, as well, considering the fact that we don't know the full truth yet."

`The guards led us to a small building with a large fence around it. On the fence were barbed wires, and there were prison guards roaming around everywhere. The guards made us walk inside the building. It smelled terrible inside, like old sweaty socks. One of the guards led us into a room that had interrogation chairs and a light that dangled from the ceiling. J and the shadow winced at the sight of the light because of how bright it was. The entire time Ophidian gave us angry glares. We ignored him and just followed the guard.

"I will be interrogating each of you one by one, starting with Ophidian." The two of them left us, and we all were left alone.

I looked over at Daniel who was eyeing me with a look of true terror on his face. Beside him, Shafty has the same look on her face.

"What's wrong?" I asked them, confused as to why they both were looking at me like that.

Daniel grabbed my arms and showed them to me. My skin had started to change from blue back to my original skin color, and instantly my heart dropped.

Liam looked at me with concern and said, "Are you okay, Jani? You look a little pale."

The guard came out of the room and asked for us to come in. While we walked into the room, Ophidian walked out with a grin on his face. He must have told more lies about us, giving me more to worry about.

After a long time of telling the guard our side of the story, he told Ophidian to stay where he was while the rest of us came into the room with him.

"Listen, I believe your story, but I can't arrest him unless you have solid proof that what you're saying is true." We all looked at one another without saying anything, because we didn't really have any proof.

"Are you feeling okay, kid? You look sick," the guard said, looking at me. He put a hand on my forehead. "You feel hot, too. We have an infirmary if you need to go there."

Then the guard really looked at me, and realized I was not one of the blue people native to Shadows Creek. With complete shock all over his face, he demanded "Who are you? How did you make it to Shadows Creek?" We had to explain the entire story from the very beginning. We told him about Autumn, a name I hadn't heard in a long time, and the note in my mailbox. We told him about the first battle with the shadows and the whole story about my mother and father trying to murder me.

After we explained the entire story, the guard just stared at us with a blank expression. His turned his gaze to me and pondered aloud, "You can't be human, you can't even be a shadow. You must be some supernatural being." He started to write something down into the little notepad of his.

Just then, Ophidian stepped inside the room with an angry glare. "Why did you help them if you were just going to betray them in the end? Your story isn't really adding up," The guard said. Ophidian looked at us with an annoyed face.

"I didn't betray them. I didn't do anything wrong," he said, obviously lying.

The snake on Ophidians hat slithered to the table. It looked like it wanted to say something, but it couldn't. It started to struggle on the desk and had a very agitated look in its eyes. Everything went black then, and we couldn't see anything. It wasn't painful and it didn't make us feel any type of negative way, but it was more of a dark calm that came over the room.

"What's going on?" the guard said angrily. "Ophidian, whatever you're doing, stop it this instant or I will put you behind bars!"

"I'm not doing anything, I'm just as confused as you are," he said. It sounded like he was telling the truth, but if it wasn't him, then who could have been doing this? Ophidian was the only one who knew how to use magic.

Finally, the dark cleared out and on the table was a small kid who looked around ten years old, with white hair and red snake eyes. His skin was a pale-white, scaly, and dry. He had a tiny crown on his head, which seemed out of place. Looking over at Ophidian, you could see that his eyes no longer looked like they belonged to a snake and are simple brown eyes. The boy on the desk was dressed in all white along with his white, long, slicked-back hair and looked directly at the guard.

"I have been with this man for at least fifty years, and I can tell you now that this man is a dirty liar. Why else do you think he has a magic shop hidden? To hide himself from others of course! Also, the reason why he couldn't leave the shop is because he was put under house arrest! Why are you even considering believing him?" the boy said with a dark raspy voice.

Ophidian looked at the boy with shock, while we gasped realizing that someone who looked that young had lived for more than fifty years. That was our proof—Ophidian's own snake went against him.

"It was one small argument! You didn't have to blow my cover like that… what is wrong with you?!" Ophidian yelled.

"If you haven't noticed, you don't have the authority to talk to me that way anymore, considering your abilities to hurt me are no longer with you," the snake person snapped back at him.

The guard said something into a speaker that no one could really understand, because no one was really paying attention him. Whatever he said made two guards burst into the room to take Ophidian away from the group. Ophidian protested and struggled against the guards, but they were able to take him away from us and put him into one of the cells. The boy glared at us and didn't say anything.

"You're older than fifty?!" Liam cried out, chuckling. "You look like a small five-year-old child!"

The short man walked over to Liam with a glare and said, "I take offense to that, and yes, I am at least one-thousand years old."

The guard that stayed with us in the room was obviously creeped out, as he left the room quickly without acknowledging the fact that we were free to leave now.

"If you don't mind, I'm staying with you from now on. I require food, water, and shelter," Daniel laughed nervously, and Shafty just groaned.

We all left the prison, but paused to look over the fence. We saw Ophidian being led into a cell while trying his best to convince the guards of his innocence. We returned to Shafty and Daniel's house, which was now the home of our entire group. It is a wonderful thing their place is huge now that we have new roommates. The snake made himself at home instantly.

"Ophidian had told you that my name was Apep right?" the snake said with a curious look. We all look at him and nod in agreement. "Well that is the name that he decided to call me when he stole my real name. It was his original name, but I'm sure you all are used to calling me Apep and calling the old geezer back there Ophidian, so don't bother calling me any other name."

We all looked at each other confused. Was there really a reason he had to tell us this?

"Why did he have to betray us though?" J asked.

"It was his plan from the first day he met you Jani. He was currently on house arrest. That's why he never left the shop and I went with you instead. The only way he would be taken off house arrest was if he gained your complete trust. He knew you would trust him once he separated Jani and J from each other. He would've gotten away with it if it weren't for you showing up at the right moment," he explained.

"Whose side are you even on?" Shafty asked, trying to comprehend the situation.

"Why I'm on your side of course. I never cared for that criminal," Apep said with a disgusted look.

We all sat around him in awkward silence. No one said a word and we all looked around in different places. It's a good thing there was enough room for Liam, J, the shadow, the little boy, Apep, Shafty, Daniel, and I. When I first met Shafty and Daniel and saw their house, I was surprised at how big it is. They had to be very wealthy to have a place that big. Daniel seemed to be fine with so many people here, if only slightly nervous, while Shafty seemed to be a bit irritated, though she didn't say anything about it.

Apep made himself comfortable in a chair. "Come on everyone and gather around. I have to tell you all a story."

Everyone sat around him with annoyed and confused faces. I was honestly uncomfortable around this guy—he gave off a weird aura.

"Do you want to hear the story of how I, Apep, became a snake?" he asked all of us.

Nobody answered him except for the shadow, who said, "Not really, no."

Apep glared at all of us and cleared his throat after a huge sigh. "Too bad, I'm telling you anyways."

Apep straightened himself in the chair. I personally thought it was funny watching him in the chair, considering his age and how his feet don't even touch the floor. I'm usually a fan of stories but the other don't seem amused.

Then Apep started his story from the very beginning, "I was born in here in Shadows Creek with a loving family. I had a love for snakes because I didn't have any siblings. One day, my parents had gone missing and never came back for at least ten years. I then decided to take care of myself and slowly resorted to dark magic. It kept me alive for a very long time, which explains my old age. Eventually I associated with Ophidian, who was a nice guy at the time with useful ideas. He also had amazing black magic skills and was my business partner." He then sighed and look disappointed. We were all interested in the story and couldn't keep our eyes off him. We were anxious to discover what happened next.

"What happened next?" The little boy interjected.

"Be patient child, I am just getting to that, but this is where things go downhill." All of us moved in closer and listened.

"After a while, Ophidian started doing illegal magic."

"What did he do?" J asked.

"He tried doing dangerous, dark magic on people. It backfired multiple times, but he still managed to kill innocent people. Then he stole amulets and jewels from famous sorcerers and was always on the run from the police. He was finally put under house arrest inside of the shop, which was also his home. He begged them to let him keep his magic tools and they let him, which was a big mistake. I came to visit him one day, and that's when I found out he was put under house arrest. We had an argument about his choices, and he used his dark magic to turn me into a snake. When he did that, I panicked and wanted him to turn me back, but I couldn't speak. He laughed and forced me to stay with him. I tried to leave multiple times, but he always found a way to hold me back. Eventually, after years of being another creature, I finally got used to it.

"That's when you and the shadow came into the store, and Ophidian came up with a plan. He took advantage of your good works in the neighborhood and took all the credit just so he could get out of house arrest. I know all about Shafty's anger issues, and suspected she would go up to him and punch him in the face, which amused me." He then laughed, while looking at Shafty who had an angry face. "After he was sent to jail, I managed to steal one of his dark magic items and turned myself back into my normal form, except I still have some snake appearances," he said, pointing to his eyes and scaly skin.

We all had listened to his stories with intrigue. Maybe life with all these roommates wouldn't be so bad after all.

Chapter Sixteen
The Frustrating Chase

IT HAD BEEN a few months and nothing bad had happened to us yet, thankfully. I finally had the ability to make my skin a normal, grayish-blue again, and the others said that they were happy to see me back to normal. I just laughed at that, which made them confused. We got used to having multiple people live at the house. Daniel was having a wonderful time cooking for everyone, and I must admit, he makes really delicious tasting food. With his own money, Liam bought the new and improved Zenith Console TV. It's the newest TV that has come out and it's fun to watch movies on.

After a while sitting around watching movies, the TV flickered and showed an emergency news clip.

"Murderer, thief, and mastermind, Ophidian the Dark Magician makes his way out of prison and is now on the run. If you see a very tall man like the one in this picture, please report to the police station immediately."

On the screen there was a picture of Ophidian, with his hair rugged and wearing a prison outfit. He had an unsettling smirk on his face and he was looking right at the camera, which made a chill run down my spine.

None of us said anything—we just sat in silence. The small boy started to well up with tears and the shadow looked like it wanted to vomit.

"What are we supposed to do now?" J said softly, with a shaking voice.

Apep didn't say anything for a while, and then he sighed and looked at all of us with a reassuring smile. "Do not worry my friends, he is most likely out to kill me, because I ratted him out, landing him in prison. I highly doubt he's coming to kill or harm any of you, so I would like you to stay calm."

If anything, that just made things worse. The little boy had tears streaming down his face and we all looked vulnerable.

On the table a small radio turned on and the voice of a prison guard talked in a deep, hoarse voice. "To all of Shadows Creek's residents, we would like you to stay indoors with the windows closed, doors locked, lights off, and stay in the far corner of your house. DO NOT make any noise. This is not a drill. This is for your safety. I'm having a hard time myself. I'm at work here in the prison and my wife and two daughters are home alone without me, I hope their safe."

The guard on the radio started sobbing until the radio cut off. Without saying anything Shafty and Daniel ran to turn the lights off, closed the curtains, and locked the door.

"Shouldn't we stop this?" Liam asked.

"We can't do anything about it until we have a plan on how we can stop him. Until then we all have to hide in the corner of the house." Daniel explained.

All of us went to the most inconspicuous corner and hid there, silently. The shadow tried its best to calm down the small boy who was sitting in its lap. All of us squeezed together as tight as we could, trying to blend in with the dark as much as possible. Shadows Creek was now silenced, and you couldn't hear a thing. No one knew where Ophidian was, or where he even could have gone. After a while, we all got tired and decided to do sleep shifts, where one person stays awake while the others are sleeping.

I took the first shift and it was starting to get lonely, which is my number one fear. I have always had monophobia ever since I was young, but I have never truly experienced it. I looked at the others. With them I didn't have to feel alone. I now had people who would risk their lives to keep me safe, and I would do the same for them if it ever came to that.

After a long time of thinking, I felt a tap on my shoulders, and I saw Shafty smiling at me.

"What are you thinking about? You look like you have a lot on your mind," she whispered so she didn't wake anyone up. I just shook my head.

"Why are you up?" I asked her.

"It's my turn to look out for anything. You should go to sleep, and you need it because the radio will be updating us on the situation tomorrow."

I laid down on the floor and looked around—it was night and the full moon was out. I was worried that we didn't know what to do yet. After a while I drifted off into a deep sleep.

I wasn't sure how long it'd been, but I woke up to Daniel shaking my shoulder. I sat up, about to say something, until I saw Apep signaling me to be silent. Everyone was huddled up and awake, except for the young boy. I listened, and outside I could hear loud footsteps walking across the sides of the house. Through one of the curtains I could see the outline of a man with a top hat full of small trinkets, which was the same hat Ophidian wore.

I looked at the outlined man in utter horror. I wanted to scream or cry, but I couldn't because he was right there looking to kill one of us. The little boy was still asleep. The others probably kept him asleep so he wouldn't panic.

Just then, we heard a loud banging on the door, which made the little boy stir a little in his sleep. Someone slid a note under the door into the house, but no one moved to picked it up yet. The silhouette outside the window then left quickly, and we all sat in fear.

"Stay here," Apep whispered to all of us.

He walked silently to the door and picked up the note. He sat back down with the rest of the group and read it. I stayed where I was while the others decided to read it with him. I didn't want to read anything. I was tired of dealing with this and just wanted things to be normal again.

The others sat in silence and I was curious why. They all looked up and stared at me with faces full of pity, worry, and of course, fear.

"What's wrong, why are you all staring at me?" I said feeling uncomfortable.

No one said anything until Apep spoke up. "It isn't me who Ophidian wants to kill Jani, it's you."

If the room could get any more silent, it did. I tried to breathe normally but I couldn't; I wanted to speak but I couldn't. Why were people always after me? What could he possibly get from me?

"Don't worry Jani, there are many people who wanted to kill you. Your mother, your father, those wild hounds, and the shadow! I'm sure we can defeat him with ease." Liam said, trying to cheer me up but obviously failing. The shadow glared at him at the mention of my misfortune.

"Why did you have to bring that up?" Daniel asked quietly.

"When we fought the shadows, we had a plan. When we fought Jani's father, we had a plan, but this time we don't have the slightest clue what to do," Shafty said.

The radio made a static noise and the panicked voice of the officer was back. "To all of the residents of Shadows Creek, we advise you to keep safe at home because the murderer is still on the loose. It has been reported the he has already killed at least thirteen residents. His demands have been reported. He demands the officers leave him alone and he is not arrested for his crimes, and he also wishes to see a resident named Jani Topia. If you know who Jani Topia is, please contact the Shadows Creek Prison, so we can get to the matter at hand. Thank you for your time, and please remember to stay put in your homes and stay hidden."

I stayed silent. I didn't want to think about anything curretly. All of this was way too much for me. We had to come up with some type of plan—it was our fault for trusting him in the first place. The radio had been static, but then a low, agitated voice started talking.

"Hello Jani, it's me, Ophidian, and I have a very important message for you, so I would like you to listen closely."

All of us looked at the radio in horror. The little boy was fully awake now and looking at the radio as well.

"I bet you're wondering why I want you, out of all people, am I correct?"

I looked at the others who looked at me with worry and fear in their eyes.

"I am no longer going to be chased by the police and I no longer have anyone coming to my shop anymore. I want you to be my personal helper now that Apep has left me," he said with an annoyed voice.

"He wasn't any help anyways, but I figure that if I turn you into any animal, you also wouldn't have any ability to leave… and no one would miss you anyways, right? You're not even the original you! So, it wouldn't even matter anyway. I can go back to my normal life like before I was put under house arrest, now that the police have agreed to leave me alone. I can go back to doing experiments on other people starting with you."

He sounded like a maniac, and I was very unsettled.

"I'm not going to let that happen," Apep said with an angered voice. "I've been his servant for years and I dreaded every second of it. All of the pain and hard work trying to keep him in a good mood, and because of all of that I promised myself that I'm never going to let anyone else go through what I had to go through." He seemed like he was talking to himself, lost in his memories enslaved to Ophidian.

"The faces of those innocent people who were about to get brutally murdered, just because of some experiment that he tried to do. I was one of the lucky ones who wasn't murdered in his experimentation process. I'm not going to let that happen to you Jani, or any other innocent person."

We all looked at him with pity and fear. Anxiety coiled up in everyone.

"If we are going to stop them, then we would need some type of plan, wouldn't we? Once we go through with the plan that means that everyone after Jani would be gone, and we would no longer have to live in constant fear, right?" J asked the group with a reassuring face, trying to cheer us up.

Daniel became nervous and picked up a phone. "There is only one person who could come here and help us, and I'm sorry for those of you who haven't met him yet."

Shafty thought for a while, and then you could see her face turn red with rage. She looked at Daniel and with a low voice said, "I beg of you, do not call him here. He will only make this problem worse."

"He's going to help us with our problem, Shafty. I'm going to call him."

"Why do you even have his number?"

"Just in case a situation like this happened. I never told you because you would have a huge fit over it."

"He's going to put even more stress on the situation than we already have."

"It's the only thing we can do now."

Daniel dialed a number and called this mysterious person while Shafty sighed in defeat. I knew who they were talking about. He's the one person Shafty loathes the most—William from the run-down weapons shop. We'd been to the moldy, rat-infested, smelly store twice already, and Shafty punched him both times.

"Who is he calling that has her so worked up?" the shadow whispered to me with concern.

"You'll feel the same way once you meet him, don't worry. He's honestly annoying in every possible way."

"I only met him once and he seems immature," Liam said, sighing.

Daniel started sweating and seemed slightly startled when William answered and said, "Hello Daniel, how are you? Did you finally ditch that so-called friend of yours for assaulting me? I'm seriously thinking about calling the authorities on her for punching me in my nose twice!"

"I'm right here, and I'm pretty sure that the authorities don't care about what happens to you, and Daniel did not ditch me, as a matter of fact." Shafty's voice sounded like she was about to start screaming. She even looked like she wanted to. Her face turned from her normal blue, to a cherry red, and she looked really tense. Her fists were clenched like she wanted to punch something. We all kept our distance.

On the other end of the line you could hear William murmuring to himself. "What do you need?" he asked in a very rude tone.

"We need you to come over here, can you do that?" Daniel asked, giving Shafty an angry glare, to which Shafty just shrugged.

"Did you not hear the radio about the murderer on the loose? I'm not leaving this place, forget about it."

No one said anything for a while until Daniel said, "What if we got you a better job?"

I listened to them talk for a while, until I heard William sigh with annoyance.

"I'm in! I'll be on my way," William said before he hung up.

The little boy sat with confusion, as well as J, Apep, and the shadow.

"So, what's the plan for when he arrives?" The little boy asked.

"He doesn't go anywhere without a bag full of weapons and that can be very useful. Ophidian has magic, which can be difficult to fight. This is where Apep comes in, because he knows the most about him. He will give us orders on what to do if Ophidian ever thinks about hurting one of us. We won't back down on Ophidian—if he dies, that's a good thing. If he gets his magic taken away from him, that would also be great, and he won't be able to escape prison again.

"Someone will have to go close to him and find a way to keep him still, so we have a better chance at doing this. This is where Shafty and the shadow come in. Shafty's tough and the shadow is great at hiding—it's a shadow, obviously. Jani, Apep, J and I will find a way to get him out of the back of the shop.

"Jani, whatever you did with your eye at the hospital where a full blast came out of it and took out each and every one of those shadows is going to be needed, if you know how to do it." Daniel explained all of this to us and we agree, except I didn't know about my eye. wasn't sure how I did that at the hospital because I was blinded.

"What am I going to do?" the little boy asked, disappointed.

"You have the hardest job of all, do you think you can handle it?" Daniel asked the little boy in a low and serious voice.

The little boy nodded and listened closely.

"You have to sit here and make sure William doesn't touch anything in this place," Daniel said laughing at the end. The little boy intensely stared at him with a pouty face.

Shafty chuckled, saying, "Trust me little buddy, you have the hardest job here. He likes to eat, sleep, touch very fragile things, and steal things that don't even belong to him." The little boy gave a huge smile, which is honestly the most adorable thing I have ever seen.

After a couple of hours, the door opened with incredible speed, and William walked in. We almost had a heart attack thinking someone broke in. He wore muddy boots and tracked a mess all over the perfectly white floor, which made Daniel sigh in frustration. William was wearing a hat and an overly large coat that was covered in the red dirt from outside. He sat on the ground next to all of us, sending dust everywhere, and driving us to move back away from him. Did he not know anything about personal hygiene? He looked at us without saying anything, like he was confused.

"Who are these people?" he asked me.

"That doesn't matter, did you bring your bag full of weapons? They will be needed for our journey," Daniel said.

"What kind of journey are you going on? You never told me what you needed these for. Are you all going after that evil magic dude?" William asked.

"Of course not," Shafty replied, lying.

"I'm going with you then."

"No, you're not," Apep stated, not bothering to look up at him.

"Who are you exactly?" William said in the rudest way possible.

Apep almost said something, but I motion for him to stop. There's no getting through to William, and it wasn't worth Apep's energy to keep going.

"I'm sorry William, but you're not coming with us. You're going to stay with this little guy right here," Daniel said, motioning towards the little boy who looked at William with disgust.

"You want me to babysit a pipsqueak?" William said with a smug look.

"Actually, it's going to be the other way around. He will oversee you, and if you even try to boss him around, I will not hesitate to break your nose for the third time," Shafty declared, returning the smug look back to him. William's smile turned into a frown and he pulled out his large bag without a word.

"Long distance or short?"

"We will be firing from behind, so I would need at least a bow and arrow for Jani, I'm certain that she's good at aiming. I'll take your bombs, and Apep and J can take whatever is comfortable for them," Daniel explained to William.

"I know long distance magic, won't be needing anything." Apep said.

"I'll take another bow and arrow if you have one," J said.

Once we have everything, William asked, "Are you guys going to pay for any of this?"

"No." I said, and we all leave the house. I hoped the little boy could handle dealing with him.

While walking outside, Liam decided to ask, "Does anyone know where we are going?" This made us all think. None of us really knew where to go.

"I would assume he's waiting for us in his shop because all of his magic things are there," Apep said.

This was going to be harder that we thought it was. We kept walking and we saw that the streets of Shadows Creek were all empty—no one is walking down the sidewalk like people usually like to do.

We made it to the shop, and all stood in front of it. Once we went in, there was a chance that some of us would get badly hurt. We hoped that wouldn't happen but were sure at least one of us would.

"Does everyone know the plan?" Daniel asked, shaking and nervous just like the rest of us. We all just nodded, too nervous to speak.

Apep opened the door slowly with a creak. Inside of the shop, the lamps that were once beautiful were now shattered on the floor, and dangerous wires were dangling from the ceiling. The walls started oozing and Shafty touched them.

"It's only oil, not blood," she said.

We all kept walking until we saw his front counter. It had papers covering the entire thing and tiny smears of blood were on a few of them.

"Those are his experiment papers," Apep stated. "They tell him which ones worked, which ones didn't, and how to make them work."

You could tell it was true, because certain papers with the word "Fail" on them were covered in dried blood and were crumbled up slightly. Ophidian must have been stressed out about the amount of fails he was getting. Served him right, honestly.

We all stood still once we heard chuckling and footsteps on the roof of the building. Before we could make a move, we all were thrown upside down to the ceiling, so hard that we all could've had concussions. It felt like being hit by one of the largest forces, but it didn't stop there.

The movement was so quick, and we couldn't process what happened fast enough, because we are suddenly thrown back onto the ground. Everything was destroyed, the roof was caved in, as the ground filled with rubble and everyone started looking around trying to see if we could find Ophidian before he did anything like that again. J spotted him from a hole in the top of the roof, and we could see him smiling with a wide and satisfied grin. Before we could do anything to him, the building started shaking and we were all thrown wall to wall, ceiling to floor. A few shards of glass made it toward my face, arms, and legs. It felt like needles poking me everywhere.

The others were struggling to focus on making it to the ceiling so they could find Ophidian, but the shop wouldn't stop tossing us to the walls, ceiling, and floor. It felt like we were there for hours until I was no longer slammed against a wall, but instead into a full body of water. It didn't look like we were in Shadows Creek anymore. I knew he had magic and all, but I didn't know he would have an ability like this.

"What's going on?" Shafty yelled from across the water.

"I don't know, I've never seen him do anything like this before, but it appears to me that we are trapped in the middle of a large storm!" Apep said.

I tried to call out to them but all I could do was try to swim toward them. The waves pushed me back while I tried to move forward.

In the distance we could see Ophidian on the top of his shop, which was sitting on a dock that seemed to go nowhere. He lifted something up into the air which had an odd shape, but I couldn't really make out what it was. He then started laughing hysterically and slammed the object down. We all blacked out.

When I opened up my eyes, I saw that there was no one near me and I was all alone. I don't like being alone whatsoever. I tried to swim my way towards a dock in the distance, trying to find the others, but it was so hard because the water was freezing and I could barely use my legs. As I swam, I couldn't help but notice something touching my ankle. I almost had a panic attack and looked in the water.

Before I could see what was touching my leg, I was pulled down underwater with a brutal force. I wasn't even sure where I was going, because whatever was pulling me wouldn't stop moving at an indescribable speed. Whatever this thing was, it must not have needed to breathe air…

Whenever I tried to move my arms or kick my feet, I only made it worse, because the creature underwater responded by tightening its grip on my leg. The only ability I had was to look at the rushing water carrying away blood from the wounds on my leg that were left from the creature tightening its grip.

Holding my breath was becoming harder and harder, and my heart was starting to beat faster and faster. I tried to fling my arms up or move so I could go back to the surface, but I couldn't do it. This, *thing*, kept pulling me deeper and deeper down into the water.

The water pressure was getting to me, and I finally realized that I was probably starting to die. I struggled even more than I did before, reacting to my immediate urge to breathe. I tried my hardest not to breathe but I couldn't take any of it anymore, and I took a large breath. Now, I knew for a fact that I was dying. I couldn't see anything clearly except my wet, black hair and blurred vision, and I couldn't really think straight. I couldn't feel anything. All I had left to do was think.

With the last of my energy, I tried my hardest to look around one more time. I didn't feel like the creature was even gripped on my leg anymore, and suddenly I saw that I was finally able to move my arms.

At least I thought so.

I looked up and I could see that I was still underwater but could breathe now. I tried to swim up to the surface and found that I could with ease. I made it there and saw a large dock, and swam my way over there, though it didn't exactly feel like I was swimming. It was more like I was floating. I made it to the dock and saw the others there, sitting and saying nothing with all their feet dangling in the water. I stepped onto the dock and sat next to them, but none of them said anything or even acknowledged the fact that I was there. I tried to tap Liam's shoulder to get his attention, but all he did was shiver, and I didn't know how to feel or what to do.

"Do you think she's dead?" Shafty asked the others. Who? Me? Did they not see me right here?

"Don't say that, she'll find her way here," Daniel said, with his voice sounding doubtful.

"Who are you talking about?" I asked all of them, but only one of them seemed to hear me. J looked around and then looked at me. Her face then lit up and she looked at the others.

"I'm going to walk around the dock for a while," she told them. She motioned for me to follow her and we walked a very long distance from the others—to the point where I couldn't see them anymore. "What happened to you?" she said with a shaky voice. She was tense and her eyebrows were furrowed.

"What are you talking about? I'm fine. I've been looking for you all."

J looked at me for a while and went through the small bag she kept on her back. She pulled out a small mirror and I tried to reach for it. Looking at my reflection I almost screamed. The thing is, I felt fine, but that was one of the problems. I shouldn't feel fine. I should be in a large amount of agony. In the mirror I had pale white skin and I had purple and blue veins all over me. My sweater no longer had its sleeves, my scarf was torn and my hair looked wet—just tangled thin strings. What scared me the most is that both of my eyes were now a very pale and faint blue.

CHAPTER SEVENTEEN
FINALLY GONE

I DIDN'T SAY anything at first, because as much as I want to panic, I can't.

"Am I dead?" I asked, without looking up at J.

"Sadly yes, Jani."

"Then how come I was able to see myself in the mirror?"

"I'm a shadow, which is sort of like a ghost in a way. So that mirror sort of helps me see myself," she said, looking at me. I looked at her and saw that she was thinking about something. Her eyes were wandering to different places.

"Jani," she started, hesitating, "do you want to have your original body back?"

I didn't respond. I did want my body back, but at the same, what would happen to J? I only nodded slowly.

"It might be dangerous," she explained, "but it's the only way that you'll be able to defeat Ophidian."

"How will it be dangerous?" I asked, curious.

"You have a gift inside of you Jani, I can easily tell. You might not feel it, but trust me, it's going to get better, but it might be difficult, to the point where your emotions might just control your actions."

I looked at her and looked far back at the others, who were staring out at the water.

"Kind of like how you made me murder the doctor and nurse at the hospital?"

She gave an awkward smile and nodded.

"Does this mean you won't be with us anymore? Will I still look like a dead person after this?"

"Sadly, it is a yes to both questions. If you get your old body back, I'll be gone but I'll be ok, and when the others see you, they're going to be frightened by your looks. Except for the shadow, though. It already knows what's going on and it's not very happy about it."

"Why not?"

She went back into her bag and pulled out a very small bottle filled with a black looking liquid. She opened it and looked at me. "It's because it doesn't want me to die, but we don't have another choice. When I die you have to possess this body, and don't try to talk me out of it because I have already made my decision."

I didn't say anything, and just watched. I agreed with her about getting rid of Ophidian, and I did want to have the original body again, so if her dying was the only way to do that, then so be it. I'll always remember her, and she was a great friend to have as well—I'll miss her. I looked over to see her lying on the dock with her eyes wide open and the small bottle, empty and laying next to her.

I wasn't sure how you're even supposed to possess a body, so this was difficult for me. I reached down to touch her, and all of a sudden things went white and I found myself looking at the gray clouds in the sky. I got up and looked around, and I wasn't sure if it worked or not. I felt like I'd been through torture, so that must have been a sign that it worked, but I wouldn't know for sure until I walked over to the others to see if they start to panic.

I ran toward them and they all looked over, standing up instantly. All of them looked horrified and I realized that I don't look like my regular self anymore. I was now a living person who looked like the undead.

"What happened to you Jani?" Daniel said, pointing at my skin and face. He was trembling, which obviously meant he feared me.

"You no longer have a green eye Jani, what happened while you were gone? Did Ophidian get to you?" Apep asked, concerned.

I glanced over to the shadow, who didn't say anything.

"I'm fine, we need to find Ophidian as fast as we can." I told them.

"You know how to stop him?" Liam asked. I just shrugged, because I honestly didn't know what I was doing. J just said that I would get angry and then something would happen, but I wasn't sure what.

We all sat on the dock again, trying to figure out a way to find Ophidian and get back to Shadows Creek. In the distance a large ship made its way toward us. We all stood and waited for it to let us on.

"I'm so happy there is someone here to find us," Liam said, relieved.

We looked around the boat, and just from a quick glance, you could tell that it was for high-class people. The floor was made of marble and the place was humongous. Everyone on the boat looked wealthy and seemed to be very high maintenance. On the other hand, we all looked like we got our clothes out of a garbage dump and were all barefoot, which was even worse.

"What are you all doing on this abandoned dock? No one ever goes here anymore," the man, who must have been the captain of the ship, questioned. He wore a very nice, dark navy-blue suit, with his hair all shaved and a long white beard on his face. On his forehead he had a large scar, which looked like it was very painful.

He must have caught me staring, because he turned to me and said, "You must be wondering where I got this scar, am I right? I should be asking the same question about you. What happened to your skin, face, hair, and eyes?"

I didn't say anything and just turned away. This guy had an unnerving feel to him, and I didn't like it at all.

"My name is Edgar Erebus, but you can call me Captain instead. Judging by your looks you have nowhere to go, would you like to work for me instead?" he said, with his hands behind his back, examining all of us very closely.

I guessed Shafty could tell how I felt because she looked at him very carefully and said, "I'm sorry to disappoint you but we do have a place to go. We just needed help and we were wondering if you could help us find our way."

The man seemed disappointed by that comment and stopped smiling. "Let me guess, you want a place to stay, right? I'm sorry but in order to stay here you'll need some type of money. I don't run my business for free."

"How about we make a deal. If you help us find our way, we will give you a load of valuable treasures?" Shafty said, looking at Edgar without breaking eye contact. The two of them were very similar, because they are both stubborn.

"What kind of valuable treasures are we talking about here? How do I know you're not just bluffing?"

"Have you ever heard of the fraud named Ophidian?"

"Of course I have! That man murdered about half of my workers. Now I'm desperate for someone to help me around here."

"So sad," Shafty said without any sympathy. "I know where everything he owns is, if you take us to where we need to go, I will take you to the riches."

Edgar thought for a while and finally said, "Deal."

"How do you know Ophidian has any riches at all?" Liam asked.

Apep stepped in before Shafty could answer. "He steals money from banks and from other people, he has a lot of cash."

"Apep, do you know how we can find out where Ophidian is hiding?" Apep sat on the ground and thought. He closed his eyes and his back was completely straight. His breath was slow and steady.

"Jani, where were you born?"

"I was born in a hospital a few miles from Suns Creek."

"Where were you born as a shadow?" he asked, opening his eyes slowly to look up at me.

"I'm not sure, the only life I've known was as a human being."

Apep looked at me and sighed. "Jani, I know what happened between you and you know who. Thankfully I was able to make them forget her, but I know that deep down you know everything about your *actual* past life," he whispered very quietly.

I stood there in shock. No wonder Shafty, Daniel, and Liam never mentioned J at all, he made them forget. I keep thinking, but I couldn't seem to remember anything.

Suddenly, just as if it was instinct, I said, "I was born in the Shadows Creek rose garden."

Apep smiled and nodded.

Edgar walked over with a more hyped-up attitude. "Have you all figured out where you would like to go? We have no time to waste."

"Do you know how to get to Shadows Creek?" Liam asked.

Edgar perked up. "Why, that isn't too far from here, we will get there before you can say hurricane." I'm not sure if that was supposed to be reassuring, but it surely wasn't at all.

While the boat started heading towards Shadows Creek, Daniel's face turned from his normal shade of blue to the brightest green—the same color he puked over the side of the boat. One of Edgar's workers took him to a room so he could be away from the actual sight of the water.

On our way, we saw a dock that led to a blood-red dirt road, which is pretty much what all the roads look like in Shadows Creek. We were close! Once we docked and were ready to leave the boat, Edgar stopped us before we can go on our way.

"No funny business. My men and I will be waiting here, and if it takes days for you to get back, we will find you, and punish you for lying to us."

We all just nodded and ran off, following Apep. Apparently, he knew where we were supposed to be going. He ran without stopping, which was sort of tiring. Once we stopped, we saw a garden full of red roses. None of them were damaged, and they all looked so beautiful.

A tall figure in the distance started to get closer and closer to us until it finally stopped and we were able to see who it was. Ophidian stood tall and proud, watching us with a smile on his face while he picked the petals off a rose. Each petal that he plucked off rotted before it even hit the ground.

You could tell that he cleaned himself up a bit after going to prison, but he still had the look of someone who had been sleep deprived.

"I'm tired of you all surviving. Jani almost died and somehow she's standing right here in front of me. I'm not entirely sure how you managed to do such a thing."

I didn't say anything. I was tired of seeing this man mess with my life. I always felt like he was silently mocking me behind my back, and it made my blood boil.

Before Ophidian could say anything else, something went right through his shoulder. Apparently Shafty threw an arrow of some sort, making Ophidian cry out in pain. His face scrunched up as he hissed in agony. He looked up, his eyebrows furrowed, and you could see the veins all over his forehead. There was sweat all over his face and he didn't look too pleased with what Shafty did.

Without any warning, the ground shook and creatures of different shapes, sizes, color and even smell, came running at a very high speed. Ophidian sat on the ground laughing like a maniac. What was strange is that the creatures didn't come near us. They started destroying the roses. The roses were trampled, and the beautiful rose garden was starting to become brown.

Shafty, Daniel, and Liam all started to look pale in the face. This was not good for them. If all of the roses died, then all of Shadows Creek would die. I wasn't sure if I wanted to go through that again.

I was tired of this, all of it. He kept trying to kill my friends. The people I called my family. He tried to kill me. Many times. I was just plain tired of it, and angry.

I walked toward the crowd of creatures that were trampling flowers. I didn't want to confront with them, so I kept walking. They weren't happy about that and ran for me.

Before one touched me, all I saw was black and my eyes felt like they were on fire, yet it didn't hurt at the same time. I never regained vision, but I kept walking, talking. I walked forward and headed toward Ophidian, who was on the ground trying to tend to the wound on his shoulder. I regained vision and looked back to see multiple creatures on the ground, dead. I didn't care that they were dead.

This must have been what J was talking about when she had the conversation with me about anger, but honestly, I couldn't care less. I was too boiled to care about anything right then. I was right behind Ophidian and saw that his back was turned toward me.

He quickly paused and turned his head with wide eyes.

"How did–"

I cut him off before he could finish his sentence. "I'm not in the mood to hear your voice right now. Or any time ever, as a matter of fact," I told him, looking right in his eyes.

"You don't scare me child," he said in the most confident voice he could make, but I could tell he was bluffing.

He stood up and looked down on me. He was way taller than me, but it seemed that he was more scared of me than I was of him. He looked behind me and mumbled something under his breath. Turning around, I saw that every single creature he had sent to trample the flowers were dead and slowly disintegrating into nothing.

My eye started twitching, and my vision became blurry. I felt like the world was spinning. I started breathing really heavy and my head was pounding. I tried to say something, but instead of words, some *thing* came out of my mouth, to the point where I felt like my mouth was filled with water. I might have been puking, I couldn't really see.

I felt hands on my shoulders pulling me back. My eyes were closed, but I couldn't seem to open them. I felt someone lightly tap my face, trying to get me to wake up, but it took a while for me to regain sight.

I sat up and looked over to see Ophidian drowning.

He was not drowning in water, but in roses. Vines started wrapping around his arms and torso, while thorns pricked his skin, making small cuts appear all over his face. Blood trickled down as the thorns squeezed him tightly. He started sinking to the bottom of all the roses, but he didn't go down without a fight. He started screaming at the top of his lungs. He tried his hardest to stay at the top, but eventually the screaming stopped, and he yielded to the bottom of the pile.

"So," Liam started, "does this mean he's finally dead?"

Apep didn't say anything, he just nodded.

We left the garden without a word. Somehow, I didn't feel bad about anything. I felt, happy, for once.

꙳

We led the ship captain, Edgar Erebus, to Ophidian's shop. It was destroyed, but there were still many valuables in there. He sent his workers to go through and pick out as many valuables they could find.

We made it back home and saw that William had given the small boy who was watching him a hard time while we were gone, so naturally, Shafty kicked him out.

This was finally over and done with, but was it really a happy ending? I was no longer my normal self. I looked dead and I couldn't walk out in public normally like this. Apep knew what to do for my appearance problems.

He decided to run his own business, rebuilding Ophidian's magic shop. He keeps it public and he doesn't use any living creatures as test subjects. He became popular very quickly, which was great, and now he lives in his own place, but comes over to visit a lot.

Shafty, Daniel, Liam, the small boy and I are now the only people living in the big house. I'm not sure if anything is truly over, it's always a mystery when you're in Shadows Creek.

ABOUT THE AUTHOR

J'Nai Coach is sixteen years old and currently lives in South Carolina. When she was nine years old, she was diagnosed with Postural Orthostatic Tachycardia Syndrome, which happens to be an auto immune disease. Because of this, she cannot do as much physical activity like everyone else, so during her free time she finds pleasure in reading books which inspired her to write one of her own.